Sculpting His Likeness

The Women of T.H.E.T.A. Book 4: Faye

By Elizabeth Borae

T.H.E.T.A.

Chapters

Prologue

Wyatt

The black iron fence before Mr. Wyatt Armstrong created a crisp contrast to the white home. It was a fashionable prospect, but seemed a disturbing metaphor for his youth, though his sister's current residence in London wasn't his childhood home. As those memories tumbled through his mind, the warm September drizzle made him damp despite the umbrella the footman held aloft.

"We're to live here, Papa?"

The high voice awoke him from his daze, and Wyatt looked down at his seven-year-old daughter, peering up at him with large, brown eyes.

"Yes, Faye, this is our new home."

His sister, Mrs. Chelsea Caldwell, and her daughter had inherited it upon her husband's death. The home had fit the gentleman, a simple, classic man with a good eye for aesthetics who'd complemented Chelsea.

"Papa, are you well?"

He mustered up a smile. *Be courageous for my brave, little lady.* "Right as a trivet. Let's go inside so you can meet your aunts and cousin."

Ordinarily, Faye would've been excited, but there'd been many upheavals in the past year, foremost her mother's death, so she was more subdued.

Faye must be exhausted. I know I am.

The butler showed them into the drawing room, outfitted in smart furnishings and well lit by a fire. Their house in Liverpool had been charming but unassuming. When his family had packed him off fifteen years ago at the age of twenty-three, they sent him away with a sizable annual allowance, but he'd settled into a simple living. Eventually, he married and had wanted to scale up since he possessed the means, but his wife, Callie, insisted they were fine. His sister's home was more of the kind in which Callie's father now lived. To Faye, it was always a trip to the grand house to see her grandpapa.

"Smells like cookies," Faye remarked.

"Knowing your Aunt Chelsea, she probably has them baked all the time."

His sisters burst into the room.

"Wyatt!" shrieked Chelsea as she rushed towards him.

He hugged her fiercely. He'd never gotten along with his brothers and was a disappointment to his parents, but his sisters seemed eager to welcome him with open arms as long as he'd mended his ways. His last incident had involved the law and magistrate, which nearly ruined Chelsea's engagement.

Miss Bonnie Armstrong gave him a long hug and then stepped back and studied his daughter. "Faye?"

"Yes, my little girl."

The sisters exchanged looks, and Wyatt hugged his daughter to him.

No matter how many times he witnessed this reaction, he never got over it, though his sisters' response was mild. Faye was a well-spoken, pretty girl, and her characteristics were much like his. She had Wyatt's brown hair, only hers was curly, his brown eyes, and her complexion was not much darker than his fair one, though it held a golden undertone. The largeness of Faye's eyes came from her mother, and Wyatt loved to pinch his daughter's round, rosy cheeks. But because her mother was of African descent, her features made some people feel Faye differed from them, and that burned Wyatt up.

"Welcome, Faye," Aunt Bonnie said warmly. "We're so happy to have you here."

Chelsea beamed. "Aren't you just the cutest thing! My Daisy is a year older than you and will be so happy to have a playmate. Would you like to meet her and have some cookies?"

Faye grinned. "Indeed, I would, Aunt Chelsea."

Chelsea offered her hand and led Faye out of the room, chattering about what new dolls they'd get tomorrow.

Bonnie shook her head. "I don't know who's more excited about the dolls, Chelsea or Faye."

Wyatt laughed. *Some things never change.*

"Faye is a beautiful child and very poised for her age. You must be quite proud of her."

"Yes, she's a good girl." He grinned wryly. "Takes after her mother."

Bonnie rubbed his arm. "It's been a troublesome time, hasn't it?"

"Callie was..." Wyatt faltered, at a loss describing how bereft he was without her.

"You're here now. We'll get through together as best we can."

CHAPTER 1

A Breath of Fresh Air

Faye

DAISY CALDWELL RAN BY eleven-year-old Faye and pulled her through the enormous, ornate doors of Oakes Hollow. Once inside, Daisy squealed as she ripped her bonnet off, revealing a head of fine, sandy-colored hair and brown eyes the same hue as Faye's. "I can't believe we're to live here now!" She paused. "I suppose that's wicked to say since we're here because Uncle Stewart is dead."

Faye shrugged, not knowing what to say about that. She was sorry for anyone to lose their life, but Uncle Stewart never paid her any attention, so she didn't feel his passing deeply. While Faye had been of the understanding that her aunts and Papa weren't very close to him either, his sudden death had left them somber.

"We've returned," Aunt Bonnie wryly announced as she, Papa, and Aunt Chelsea walked in behind them. Aunt Bonnie looked much like Papa, while Daisy had inherited her lighter hair and sun-kissed complexion from her mother and strongly resembled her. Papa and his two sisters had been here briefly after the funeral, so her aunt's comment struck Faye as odd, but she supposed this return was more significant.

"I can't believe I'm back here." Papa exhaled.

Aunt Chelsea chuckled. "You two make it sound like a death sentence. It wasn't so bad, and things will be completely different with Wyatt in charge and the girls here. Come on, chin up!" She flung her arms wide. "We're embarking on an epoch."

Papa gave his sister a look as Faye and Daisy giggled.

Aunt Chelsea always makes things diverting and delightful. Faye twirled in the vast foyer. She'd never been in a room so large, and it was just their entranceway.

"On the few occasions our family held events, we'd entertain guests here since the space is so large," Aunt Bonnie said. "There's a wonderful cross breeze when the front and back entrances are open on very warm summer days."

Aunt Chelsea grabbed Faye and Daisy's hands. "I'll show you the suite Bonnie and I shared."

They ran up the stairs, across the balcony, and through a door at the end of the hall.

"Here we are!" Aunt Chelsea collapsed on a bed.

Everything was decorated in white and lilac in this bedroom, which perfectly suited Aunt Chelsea.

Faye looked out the window. The sun had appeared, and the wet gardens looked like they were sparkling. They were filled with colors and all sorts of plants, trees, sculptures, archways, and paths. "This room is lovely," she whispered as she took in the expansive landscape.

She was pleased to see that Oakes Hollow had a different wonderfulness than London. Faye liked their home in London ever so much and was hesitant to leave. For four years, they were such a merry party, and that offered some comfort after Mama had died.

When Papa had unexpectedly inherited Oakes Hollow, he warmly invited her aunts and cousin to move with them, and they accepted. Faye was glad their unique family arrangement would stay intact, for she wasn't sure what to expect of society here. New places and people made her anxious, and her father's unease increased her own.

The girls ran into the adjoining room.

"This one is larger," Daisy said. "I like it."

"Then you shall have it," Aunt Chelsea said, following them inside. "Faye, dear, would you like my old room?"

Faye nodded vigorously. Aunt Chelsea's room was much prettier.

"Faye and Chelsea will stay in this suite if you approve," Aunt Chelsea said to Papa as he walked in.

"Perfect," he replied. "That was simple."

"Papa, are we very rich, then?" Faye asked. "I feel like a princess."

Aunt Chelsea kissed her forehead.

"We have more than a few pounds, yes," he answered. "Would you and Daisy like a long walk outside? I can show you my old spots."

Faye squealed.

Aunt Bonnie ran in breathless. "Lord Yardley calls upon you, Wyatt."

Papa's eyes widened. "I didn't expect to meet him so soon. I'm sorry, girls, for we'll have to postpone our walk until tomorrow."

Faye was disappointed, but this visit sounded important, and tomorrow was soon enough.

"Do I look all right? Will I embarrass you?" Papa teased his sisters.

Aunt Bonnie gave him a playful hit on the arm. "You're fine. Now go down and represent the new regime."

*****

The girls were with Aunt Chelsea in the morning room, enjoying refreshments. They weren't horribly far from London, but it had been a busy and momentous day, and the three were hungry.

Aunt Bonnie poked her head in. "Lord Yardley asked to meet the girls."

"That's quite kind of him." Aunt Chelsea put her napkin on a small end table. "Let's not keep the marquess waiting."

Faye had been in the presence of only a couple of noblemen, and she'd never been introduced to one. "Is Papa suddenly a very important man?" Faye asked her aunt as they left the room.

"To some, he might now seem so." Aunt Chelsea was unusually solemn. "But he won't change, and those who know and love him will recognize that."

Faye was pleased with that answer. She loved her Papa just as he was.

Aunt Chelsea stopped walking and studied the girls. "We Armstrongs aren't bottom of the barrel."

Daisy giggled. "I never thought the Caldwells were."

"You're an Armstrong too, and our wealth and estate rival most noblemen." Aunt Chelsea gave them a pointed look. "You two are the daughters and granddaughters of gentlemen. Don't forget that, even if others do."

Faye and Daisy exchanged looks.

Head held high, Aunt Chelsea continued walking and the girls followed. They entered the drawing room, and Faye stopped short, taking in the space with wonder. It had an attractive prospect towards the garden and was richly furnished.

"Faye!" Aunt Bonnie said urgently.

She snapped to attention.

A tall, slender man, whom Faye supposed was Lord Yardley, chuckled gently.

"Curtsy." Aunt Bonnie gave her an exasperated look.

Faye dropped into a low curtsy. She must have missed her introduction.

Daisy started giggling as Faye stared at the floor. This was a terrible beginning.

Lord Yardley crouched in front of her, his gray eyes twinkling. "It's an attractive room, isn't it, Miss Faye?"

"Yes, it is, sir," Faye replied. "I apologize for my impertinence. I'm generally much more attentive."

Lord Yardley's smile widened. "I'm delighted to have made your acquaintance. I believe we'll become good friends."

Faye grinned and curtsied again, but this time with more enthusiasm. "I'd like that."

This man doesn't look at me differently. We'll be just fine.

Lord Yardley stood and directed his attention towards Papa. "You'll have to bring the girls over. Clive was just complaining he has no one to play with."

Papa shook his hand. "I will, and thank you."

"I believe you and your family will be a breath of fresh air around here."

*****

It was a pleasantly warm day for late spring, and Faye tried to enjoy the ride to Yardley. The sky was clear with abundant sunshine and the countryside picturesque and peaceful. Nestled amongst green hills was the mansion proper, larger than Oakes Hollow.

Faye's nervousness had lessened since she'd met Lord Yardley the day before, but she didn't know what to expect of his wife and son. Daisy held her hand as they entered the massive, stately home that announced to visitors the Fitzpatricks were an established, important family.

Lady Yardley was just as kindly as her husband, and she introduced them to Clive, who was only a couple of years older than Faye. He was a nice-looking boy with brown hair, gray eyes, and a quick smile, like his father. Clive had diversions written all over his being, and Faye and Daisy began a game of hide and find with him. They played together swimmingly, and it felt like Faye had known him all her life, even though they'd just met.

She ran into a room and crouched down next to a small table. *He'll never find me here.* Something scraped the floor next to Faye, and she screeched.

A tuft of golden hair poked out underneath the tablecloth.

Faye tentatively lifted the cloth and stared into the greenest eyes she'd ever seen. "Who are you?"

"Who are you?" the boy, who looked her age, asked back. "I live here."

"My name is Faye, and I'm playing hide and find with Clive."

Clive burst into the room and tackled her. "Got you! You're it."

Faye laughed and regained her balance. "Would you like to play with us?" she asked the green-eyed boy.

He glanced at the oversized book on the floor in front of him. "I'll stay here, thank you."

Faye sat next to him under the table. "What are you looking at?"

"Pictures," he responded softly.

"Why would you want to look at boring, old books?" Clive asked.

Faye looked over the green-eyed boy's shoulder. "These are pretty."

Clive peered over the top of the book and snickered. "No wonder you're looking at it under the table. Those are the naughty art pictures Grandpapa said we shouldn't look at until we're older."

The other boy glared at him.

"I see nothing wrong with it," Faye said. "She's just on a swing. It looks incredibly diverting."

"Maybe not that one." Clive turned the page.

"Oh," said Faye.

"That's definitely not the type of diversions we're supposed to have." Clive started making kissy faces.

Green-eyed boy slammed the book shut.

"Your turn to count, Faye. But I have to find Daisy first." Clive ran out of the room.

"I didn't mean to ruin things for you," Faye said to the other boy.

"I'm not..." He frowned. "Bad or debauched or anything."

"Of course not. I didn't think that."

"Clive made me sound like—"

Faye waved a hand. "I didn't pay him any attention. I imagine he's quite silly which should make him a fun and delightful playmate."

The boy chuckled. "He is." His grin faded. "Or used to be. I believe he's bothered by me now."

"I can't imagine anyone being bothered by you. You seem quite nice."

He gave her a shy smile. "You as well." He started leafing through the book again. "It's amazing people can dream up and make such things."

Faye pointed to a picture of a colossal sculpture. "I want to do that one day."

"I can't wait to see it."

"Are you sure you don't want to join us? You'll make four, and that's a grand number for hide and find."

He grinned. "All right then."

"I'll stay here and count."

The boy started towards the door.

"What's your name?" Faye called after him. "I assume you're Clive's brother."

He nodded. "Geoffrey. Just call me Geoff, if you please, Miss Faye."

She giggled. "You can leave off the miss. That won't do between friends."

Geoff beamed. "You're perfectly right."

*****

Geoff ran out of the room thinking about the lovely girl with huge, brown eyes who would make magnificent, gargantuan sculptures.

Faye is going to change things.

CHAPTER 2

The Sculptress

Faye
12 years later

FAYE STOOD BACK and surveyed her work, wiping her hands on the dusty-rose sculpting overcoat she wore. Grandfather Sabo's sculpture-in-progress sat upon a large cutting board on an old dresser. Rough sketches hung from a board resting against an easel, and tools lay on the table next to it.

Grandfather Sabo was a proud, distinguished man, and she was having difficulty capturing those qualities. She'd been formally schooled in the sculpture arts and possessed the skills to capture her subjects' physical characteristics. But Faye sought to convey their personality to make her pieces live, which was more challenging.

She was thrilled Grandfather Sabo made the request this past spring for his likeness from the neck up. In this piece, Faye wished to incorporate characteristics she had loved about Mama that her grandpapa possessed.

Papa spent a small fortune on her materials and arranged for this space to be her studio. It was a large, white room with high ceilings, well lit as it was in a wing that protruded from the rest of the house, allowing for windows on three walls.

Daisy breezed in and plopped onto a nearby stool. "I'm bored and in need of entertainment."

Faye grinned as she applied some slip to the side of her grandfather's head. "We aren't entertaining?"

"Aye, everyone is diverting enough, and I love you all, but I need something new."

Daisy always amused, and Aunt Bonnie had said she reminded her of Papa when he was younger. Her cousin didn't seem inclined towards marriage yet, but she had little difficulty finding others, including Faye, to join her in pleasure-seeking adventures.

"I thought you were helping Aunt Chelsea with the summer ball plans," Faye remarked.

"Yes, but I want to be entertained, not provide the diversions."

The Armstrongs hosted several gatherings annually, and one of them was an end-of-winter ball. It was a good way to keep the family occupied during the winter months, Aunt Chelsea and Daisy especially. This year, Aunt Chelsea was ill for a good portion of the winter, so they decided on a summer ball instead.

"The card party at Spalding will be within a week," Faye said. "That's something different."

"Yes, and Clive is always famously droll, so I'll look forward to that. Mum sent me to fetch you for dinner. She figured you'd lost track of time."

Faye had, and she needed time to prepare. Papa wasn't fussy, but he liked everyone properly dressed for mealtimes. He had ensured her wardrobe was amply able to accomplish the task with plenty of pretty dresses and other apparel. She cleaned up, taking off her apron, washing her hands, and wiping the dust from her hair. Her curls were soft, thick, brown ringlets that sat neatly past her shoulders. She pulled some up and back.

A half-hour later, the Armstrongs were seated for dinner. Papa never had the leaves put in the oval table when it was just them, so they were a touch tight, but he enjoyed the closeness. They were busy for a while, passing food and chattering, eager to eat.

"Papa, would you sit for me so I can make some sketches?" Faye asked between bites. "I need assistance with Grandfather Sabo's bust."

She'd done a few quick sketches of her grandpapa when they'd visited, but now that Faye had a better idea of her composition, she required some different views.

"I'd be delighted," Papa answered. "If you wish to make a more precise study, I can also arrange an escort and the carriage for a short visit to Liverpool."

"I'll consider that. Thank you."

"Speaking of visits, we've received a dinner invite from Lord Yardley," Papa announced.

Exclamations of joy resounded around the table. The Fitzpatricks entertained many guests, so the Armstrongs received formal dinner invitations from them only a few times a year. The two families enjoyed a more informal association by calling on each other almost weekly.

After dinner, Faye worked on the sketches of her father in her studio.

"I had another comb made for you," Father informed her. "The teeth are wider and the handle more substantial. I think you'll like it."

Papa fussed over Faye's tresses more than she did. Right after Mama had died, Papa braided Faye's hair every morning like her mother had, with two large

pigtails down her back. The first few were a mess
— bumpy and lumpy with strands hanging out. But
she'd loved that Papa had tried and wore those messy
braids proudly. Eventually, his hair braiding technique
became impeccable. She thought he'd asked a few local
women in Liverpool to show him. Mama had been
particular about what recipe she used in her hair, and
Papa sent special overseas for the oils and ingredients
she had used. Grandfather Sabo sold the surplus in his
shop.

Faye sighed. Her sketch wasn't coming out well
because she was deliberating on which dress would
look best for the dinner instead of concentrating on
drawing. The candles were low, and she didn't want to
arrange new ones to be lit this evening. "Thank you,
Papa, but I believe that's enough for tonight."

The Fitzpatrick Men

Geoff

CLIVE WAS AT YARDLEY for dinner the third time this week. It was beyond Geoff why his older brother came over to eat so often. Clive lived at Spalding, and it wasn't like the place didn't have a capable kitchen staff.

"Hello, brother." Clive clapped him on the back.

Geoff felt himself retreating. "Good evening."

He tried to right his attitude. *Maybe dinner tonight with Clive won't be so annoying, and I'll make it through with my sanity intact.* Deep down, he loved his brother and wasn't sure why his mere presence rankled him so much lately.

"You need to help me hide from Richard," Clive declared, plopping on the couch in the drawing room.

Clive rarely hid from his closest friend, Richard Jarvis, Duke of Hartwell. Geoff liked him as well and they were longtime friends, though Clive and Jarvis were closer.

"If you plan on being present for your own card party next week, that might be difficult," Geoff remarked. "Why would you want to hide from Jarvis?"

"Ever since his last courtship debacle, he's been almost obsessed with T.H.E.T.A."

Geoff nodded. That had been a messy bust-up several months ago.

"Richard is stretching himself thin, overseeing the expansion of the mills in Derbyshire and Thurston's enterprises." Clive studied him a moment. "You might be helpful there."

Geoff tried to keep his face neutral as he headed for the door. "I believe it's time for dinner."

He was searching for a worthwhile occupation. The Fitzpatricks had a legacy in investment and banking, and Geoff had turned his allowance into a nice cache. But he'd rather have something to set him apart from his family and give him some kind of purpose and identity other than a wealthy son of a marquess.

On the surface, this enterprise seemed to be a way to do so, but Geoff suspected Jarvis hadn't worked out the details, and that was what frequently hung people. His friend's enthusiasm and conviction sometimes propelled him to roll over others, for he was used to having things happen as he wished. That mindset wasn't too different from the brothers, but Jarvis acted unaware of it, whereas Geoff tried to keep that thinking in check.

They entered the dining room for the regularly appointed dinner time. Geoff and his brother sat across from one another at the table with his parents at either end. Like the rest of Yardley, the dining room was quiet, and Geoff relaxed into his meal. For a little while, there were only the sounds of silverware clinking the dishes.

"I've invited the Armstrongs for dinner in ten days," said his father, Lord Yardley, breaking the silence.

Geoff perked up. He liked the Armstrongs, especially Faye. He'd been in love with her for years.

"Lady Girnwood will join us as well, along with her brother and daughter," his father continued.

Geoff was less excited about their company, though he could sympathize with his father acting kindly towards a widow and her daughter. After Lord Girnwood's death over a year ago, they moved in with Lady Girnwood's brother, a baron who lived near Oakes Hollow. Geoff wasn't close to the baron, but he didn't have any problems with him either.

Though they were an attractive pair, The Dowager Lady Girnwood rubbed Geoff the wrong way, and he suspected her daughter, Lady Helena Gillingham, was attempting to set herself up with either him or Clive. She'd probably prefer Clive since he'd inherit the title and estate, but could settle for Geoff since he'd receive a large inheritance as well.

Geoff turned his mind towards Faye, a more agreeable daydream. Smart and lively. Talented and lovely.

And she liked Clive. Why see Geoff when Captivating Clive was around?

While frustrating, Faye and Clive were almost like kindred spirits, so forming that sort of attachment was understandable. Clive's close friendship with Faye was one of the few things for which Geoff admired him, but then his brother was too dense to appreciate she cared for him.

"Geoff, I was thinking of shooting tomorrow if you're available," Father said.

His father was kind, but with what would Geoff have to occupy himself? He was generally freeish. "Of course. Just name the time."

Clive frowned. "I'm available too, Father."

"You're welcome to accompany us, if you wish," he replied. "I just didn't think you'd be interested."

He usually isn't, but he's got to steal my thunder all the time.

"I'd be happy to come," Clive said.

Geoff stifled a sigh. *Another day with Clive.*

✳✳✳✳✳

Early the next morning, Geoff, his father and brother set out with Father's two dogs for the hour ride. His father enjoyed shooting more for the company than to hunt, but Geoff prized the ability to feed himself if ever necessary and had taken great pains to learn each step of the process and execute it well. This wasn't Clive's favorite activity and only took part if everyone else did.

Clive spoke about his business ventures with Father during the trip. Once they reached their destination, Father turned his attention towards Geoff as they began walking through grassland to reach the woods beyond. "What have you been up to, Geoffrey?"

"Not much, Father."

Clive ran to catch up with them. "I tried to persuade him to help with T.H.E.T.A."

Geoff exhaled. *Thanks a lot, Clive.*

"That sounds like a good idea. You don't like the venture?" his father asked.

"It seems a little patchy right now."

Clive frowned. "Just because it's not the efficient, well-oiled machine you like to associate with doesn't mean it's patchy and shoddy."

"I never called it shoddy," Geoff snapped. "And I believe patchwork is an appropriate description of what Jarvis is putting together. Different men from separate companies in various industries forming an association of sorts."

"Sounds like a patchwork to me," their father commented. "That's not to say it won't be successful."

"Exactly," Clive agreed, swatting at a tall patch of grass. "It'll work."

"I didn't say it wouldn't," Geoff said. "But I'd rather strengthen a solid framework than become one of the joints holding things together, and I'm not convinced you fellows have that yet."

Clive narrowed his eyes. "That's all right. You can ride my coattails on this one too."

Geoff stopped dead in his tracks. "Excuse me?"

"Complaining about not having an occupation, and when the opportunity comes, you hide."

"In case you haven't noticed, I've been trying to get off your so-called coattails for a while now," Geoff retorted. "Who was the one who wanted to room with the other while in London this past spring?"

"Boys!" their father exclaimed. "This was supposed to be a pleasant day together." He shot Clive a look. "Why did you come if you were just to argue with your brother?"

"I'm sorry," Clive replied.

"And give Clive's offer serious thought, Geoffrey. He's never done you harm."

"Yes, Father."

"Let's pick a suitable spot." Their father began walking again, entering the woods proper.

The two brothers glared at one another and then started after him.

In a way, his father's words about Clive were correct, which was why Geoff's building resentment towards his brother was troublesome. Geoff felt like Clive kept him partially eclipsed on purpose, and while he'd been content being overshadowed as a young boy, it seemed to be creating animosity as young men.

"I'd like you boys to call on the Armstrongs within the week," their father said as he dodged a low branch. "Find out what in particular they'd like to eat and do. I want to see to their comfort."

Father seldom fussed over his other guests like this, but he enjoyed Mr. Armstrong's company and thought highly of the entire family. Mother often called on the older sister, Miss Bonnie Armstrong, and Geoff certainly wanted to make sure Faye was happy.

"Of course, Father, we can see to that on Wednesday," Clive responded.

Geoff was annoyed that Clive had spoken for his time like that, but as usual, he had nothing planned, so it was ultimately of no matter.

"Your mother seemed concerned about Miss Faye's preferences."

"I could tell you that right now," Clive said off-handedly.

Geoff rolled his eyes. "Yes, but it's nice to be attentive towards one."

"Precisely, and when your mother inquired if she was courting anyone at present, I had no idea," explained Father. "I assumed Wyatt would have mentioned something and inquired after the gentleman if she was. Do you boys have any information? You keep much closer company with her."

Clive shook his head. "She hasn't told us anything, and I haven't noticed her pay particular regard towards anyone."

Geoff gaped at him. *How daft can he be?*

"She seems completely absorbed in her sculpting at present," Clive continued. "And it's not as though she must be married to be comfortably situated."

"That's true," his father agreed. "I believe at present Wyatt will leave Oakes Hollow to her."

Geoff was surprised. It wasn't titled, so Mr. Armstrong wasn't bound to those stipulations, but that was an unusual move. "I thought that even if there was no male heir, he'd leave it to his sisters."

"I thought that too," his father admitted. "But perhaps he reasoned Faye would see to their comfort, and you know how he is about his daughter. I have no problem with his choice; it's just not customary." He grinned. "But then Wyatt has never been bound to custom."

"Oakes Hollow would be a handsome inducement for a suitor," Clive remarked.

Geoff frowned as he sidestepped a large tree root. "No suitor should need an inducement to court Faye."

"Of course not," Clive agreed heartily. "Faye is grand. It's just another excellent enhancement."

His father chuckled. "I'm not sure she'd like to be described in such a way."

"Faye knows how highly I regard her," Clive said. "After Richard, she's one of my closest friends. If she's searching for a suitor, I'd be happy to set her up with any of my closest chaps."

"I'm sure Faye can take care of herself, and you've got enough on your plate already," his father said. "Shall we discuss how close you are to getting married?"

"I'm on it, Father," Clive assured him. "Don't worry about a thing."

"I'll try," their father replied dryly.

"I'm further along than Geoff," Clive commented. "He hasn't even courted a lady yet."

Geoff scowled at him.

"Geoffrey isn't the next marquess," his father countered.

Yes, I'm not as important.

"I thought I was fussy." Clive smirked at Geoff.

Geoff had a few standards — who didn't? Faye set a high bar, but he also hadn't met anyone he liked as much. His biggest fear was he'd fall in love and marry someone who, deep down, didn't love him back. He knew Faye wouldn't act in that manner, and he trusted her. Geoff hoped she'd change her mind about Clive and finally see him.

"Is there a young woman you've set your sights on, Geoffrey?" Father asked, his countenance kindly.

Geoff gave him a weak smile. "All this talk of ladies." He patted his father's shoulder. "Let's turn our minds towards what we've come out to do."

Clive shook his head. "Geoff would prefer to hunt instead of talking about the ladies."

Yes, it's much less perplexing.

CHAPTER 4

Friend Island

Faye

FAYE RUBBED HER EYES. She had difficulty forming noses, and Grandfather Sabo's didn't look right. Or more correctly, it was an attractive nose, but it didn't resemble his.

She took a guilty glance around her studio at the many partially finished sculptures sitting on tables, in bookcases, and on shelves. It was hard to stop herself from attempting to perfect things. Faye demanded excellence from herself, and she wanted to ensure no one found justifiable fault with her since some created plenty of reasons on their own. It was unlikely she'd need to work to provide for herself, especially if she married within her station, but she wanted to be occupied with tasks that would bring beauty and joy to others. And a little awe would be gratifying as well.

Given her propensity not to finish projects, she wanted to ensure this one didn't share the same end. Not that her grandfather would allow that. He was kind towards her, but intelligence wasn't the only quality he possessed that led to his becoming a successful businessman.

Aunt Bonnie took a seat just as Faye tackled the nose issue again.

"You look as though you're on a mission," Faye remarked.

"Yes. I took a peek in your bottom drawer."

Faye grimaced and busied herself with the sculpture.

"You can't hide from me. That chest is shamefully empty."

"You know I don't care for needlework."

"You may undergo a change of heart when you have your own home and family and wish for some of the items that chest could have provided."

"Can't I just buy those things?"

"I'm afraid your father has indulged you far too much." Aunt Bonnie exhaled. "Yes, but why run up the bills when, with a little exertion, you can make pieces yourself with your own personal touch?"

Faye made a face.

"Or work with the staff," Aunt Bonnie continued. "Your father has outlaid the extravagant expense of having an in-house seamstress. You'll appreciate having made your own things, especially being the art girl that you are."

There was truth in that. Everything Faye had she somehow made uniquely hers.

"If you're desperate to escape the actual needlepoint and sewing, your Aunt Chelsea and I would give you gifts from this home if you noticed enough to ask." Aunt Bonnie gave her a look. "There really is no excuse for this."

Faye sighed. "I'll pay more attention to it."

"Are you not desirous to be married, Faye?" Aunt Bonnie asked gently. "Most girls your age have been eagerly working on their chests for years."

Faye played with a curl. Marrying well was of utmost importance and frequently separated from marrying for love, which didn't sit well with her. Faye wished for a marriage like her parents, even though many wouldn't have approved of her father's choice of wife.

"I don't seek matrimony for the sake of just being married," Faye answered carefully. "I don't feel I lack anything."

"You do have much, and I'm pleased you appreciate that. But many young women in your station would work towards a title or sorely lament the absence of a mother."

"I do miss Mama," Faye said. "But you and Aunt Chelsea have been wonderful to me. I love my family and consider myself fortunate."

"We may not always be as we are," her aunt remarked softly.

"I know." The conversation was taking a sober turn. Faye tried to bring them back to good humor. "To be truly in love with someone would be a completely different circumstance. I'd marry him in a second."

Aunt Bonnie smiled. "There's no one you've taken a liking to?"

"I have, but we seem to be marooned on friend island right now."

Her aunt chortled. "Shall I ship you and your mystery gentleman so you can leave?"

"Please do."

"Why don't you walk with me into town this afternoon? We can visit Greenleys and get started on your chest."

Faye knew that tone. It wasn't a question. "That sounds fine, Aunt Bonnie. I'll clean up and change so we can leave."

*****

Geoff

Geoff was reading a book in the Galleria on hunting bows he'd borrowed. It was a pleasant space with family pictures and artwork. Benches were placed in between the windows that lined the hall, so it was a comfortable space to read and relax. This was Geoff's favorite area of the house.

His mother sat next to him on the bench. She was a willowy woman with hazel eyes and brown hair turning white. Geoff's looks appeared to be an anomaly, though his mother had said his features resembled a great uncle of hers.

The Fitzpatricks had a couple of notable pieces, but Mother had acquired more works and made it a gallery. They received visitors regularly, asking to see the display. Between Oakes Hollow's gardens and their painting collection, it had become a thing to stop in this part of the country for a day to tour.

"I would like to ask a favor if you're not occupied this afternoon," she said.

Geoff closed his book. He enjoyed doing things for Mama, as her engagements were usually interesting. Plus, he just liked his mama a great deal and wished to please her. "Not at all. What would you like me to do?"

"I purchased a few Hogarth paintings, the marriage series prints." She smirked. "They could serve as a lesson for you and Clive."

Geoff chuckled. "And when should we schedule our first session?"

"Judging by Clive, as soon as possible," she replied wryly. "I could almost picture him in one or two of the scenes."

"And what of father's request to purchase a work by one of the greats?"

"Ah yes, I keep pressing him as to what he means by that and told him to just choose what delights his eye. It's incredible how easily one generation's genius becomes the next one's ordinary artist and vice versa. Back to the matter at hand; I had frames made, and they're supposed to come by way of Greenleys. Would you be so kind as to go into town and check on it for me?"

"Certainly. If they've arrived, should I bring them back or send for the servants?"

"We can arrange for proper transport from the shop. I think it'd be easier."

"Very good. I'll see to it immediately."

"Thank you, son. Your father mentioned having you boys sit for a painter. A work to match the one of you as children now that you're both adults."

It would be a fine idea if he wasn't so rankled by Clive. "Is Father to make the arrangements?"

"Yes, if he goes through with it. And of course, you're free to commission your own personal likeness."

A half-hour later, Geoff stood in front of the curricle and phaeton, debating which to take. The phaeton was more like what a young man of his station would drive. *I just want to be comfortable.* He had the curricle readied. It should be a pleasant trip into town on this sunny day, and maybe he'd see if there were any new books in the shop.

The shopkeeper greeted him enthusiastically when he walked in, and Geoff inquired after his mother's frames, which had arrived. They discussed transporting them back to Yardley.

As Geoff perused the shelves, the door sounded again, and Faye and her Aunt Bonnie entered.

Geoff froze. *I can be with Faye, even if it is brief.*

The sun shone through the open door and made her brown hair glow with a red-gold cast. She wore a deep blue bonnet and a matching delicate, short-sleeved jacket. Faye had pretty brown eyes framed by long dark lashes and a smooth, soft looking complexion.

Just say hello. It's not complicated. You do it all the time.

She and her aunt had a brief conference, and then Faye walked towards the far wall. She reached for something on a high shelf.

Here's a way to occupy myself on her behalf.

*****

Faye

"Allow me to get that for you," a male voice said behind Faye.

An arm reached above her, grabbed the cloth she was attempting to retrieve, and then handed it to her.

Faye turned.

"Geoff!" she exclaimed. "I mean Mr. Fitzpatrick," she corrected, remembering where she was. "I should have known your voice. Thank you."

"You're very welcome."

She enjoyed Geoff's company, even if it was a completely different experience than her mad-cap times with Clive, for Geoff was quiet and kept to himself. A pleasant-looking boy, Geoff's features were more striking now though she preferred Clive's fetching looks.

"What brings you here?" Faye asked.

"Mother requested I see to a frame order she put in a month ago."

"How is your mother?"

"Very well. Thank you."

"And your father?"

"He is well also."

Faye tried not to laugh. Geoff was never one for extensive conversation. "Our family was thrilled to receive his dinner invitation. I'm excited to come."

"I'm looking very forward to having you." He paused. "All of you." Geoff indicated towards the bolt of cloth in her hand. "I see you are to sew."

"Yes, Aunt Bonnie convinced me that if I'm to keep a house, the sculptures won't provide warmth or cover the windows, tables, and so on and so forth, and encouraged me to make those things instead of running astronomical debts buying it all."

"Is that event in your near future?" he asked quietly.

"Not specifically. I just assume I'll be married one day."

Aunt Bonnie joined them and smiled warmly at Geoff. "What a delightful surprise running into you here."

"The pleasure is all mine, Miss Armstrong," Geoff replied. "Would you two ladies like to be escorted home? It'll be a bit tight in the curricle, but I believe we could manage just fine."

Faye and her aunt exchanged happy glances.

"That would be lovely," Aunt Bonnie replied. "Thank you, Mr. Fitzpatrick."

He took Faye's cloth from her. "And I'll see to this as well."

Faye's mouth dropped open. "You don't have to do that, Geoff—"

"It'd be my privilege."

"Thank you."

Geoff tended to the items at the counter and then offered his arm to Aunt Bonnie.

His curricle was a sharp, black one. He helped Aunt Bonnie and Faye into it, and then he climbed in beside her. After checking to make sure they were all settled, he flicked the reins, and then they were off.

*****

Geoff

Geoff took a deep breath to steady his nervousness. Maybe I should have taken the phaeton. But then I probably couldn't have fit all three of us since it's smaller and more rounded, so this was the best choice after all. "I apologize that our mode of transport isn't more comfortable."

"This is wonderful!" Faye exclaimed. "Much nicer than on foot."

"I'm sure you benefited from the exercise," Aunt Bonnie commented wryly. "Your father would probably carry you everywhere if he could."

Geoff was thrilled to offer them a ride home, and without Clive. He had Faye all to himself, snug and cozy next to him. Geoff was happy he potentially had Faye's undivided attention, but now he needed to talk.

Talking wasn't something that came naturally to him, and often it felt safer to keep his mouth shut. He didn't necessarily seek solitude or even complete silence, but companionable tranquility was the state he preferred.

He knew he was in the minority with that preference, and Faye, in particular, would like conversation. He tried to exert himself to do better than in the shop.

Geoff mulled over how to pose questions without making Faye feel interrogated. He had difficulty striking that balance, and the questions he especially wanted answers to he couldn't ask. *What kind of house would you like to keep? Large? Small? In the meadow? By the ocean? In town? What do you seek from a husband? Why Clive and not me? Do you think you'll change your mind?*

"You're deep in thought, Mr. Geoffrey," Aunt Bonnie commented. "Is anything the matter?"

He jumped. *I'm off to a great start.* "My apologies. I was just thinking of a question to ask."

Faye laughed. "And it takes that much effort? Come now, Geoff. You're amongst friends. It shouldn't be so difficult. And if you don't wish to speak, then don't. We know you're a quiet man by nature."

"Thank you, you're very generous. But I should practice and develop the art of conversation." Geoff grinned at her. "I know you'll be a very able partner."

Faye gave a mock gasp. "Why Geoff, are you teasing me? I do believe you're better at this art of conversation than you'd have us believe."

"I suspect Mr. Geoffrey is a treasure trove of observations and opinions not shared," Aunt Bonnie remarked.

"A treasure trove? You give me too much credit." Geoff smiled at Faye. "Are you ready to plunder?"

"I have my shovel and will commence digging," Faye declared. "Tell me, Geoff, what are your true thoughts on the London season?"

"You like to live dangerously, Faye. My true thoughts may scandalize your sense of propriety."

She snorted. "I doubt that, and I've heard the more difficult treasure is more worth the earning."

"Yes." He paused. "So, my true thoughts on the London season..."

The three had an entertaining conversation about what they liked and didn't during their stays in London.

He stopped in front of Oakes Hollow and handed the women out of the curricle.

"Faye, I'll head inside if you'd like to thank and say goodbye to Mr. Geoffrey properly." Aunt Bonnie gave Geoff a smile.

Like she knows... Geoff cleared his throat.

"I'm sure I won't be but a minute." Faye turned towards him and patted his hand. "Now, was that so bad?"

I could definitely get used to having her undivided attention more often. He held her hand for a moment. "No, I enjoyed it quite a bit."

"Excellent. Give your parents our best wishes and tell Clive he was missed."

Geoff felt like he got doused with ice-cold water. *Of course, Faye missed Clive.* He dropped her hand and bowed. "I will. Have a lovely evening."

"You too, and thank you again." She held up the package from the shop.

Geoff watched Faye disappear into the house.

Clive. Even when he's not here, he is.

CHAPTER 5

The Card Party

Faye

FAYE GAVE CLIVE a bright smile as he settled her into a seat at his card party. Spalding was a mini castle, complete with a tiny moat. It fit Clive's personality well — a grand mix of enchanting with bachelor diversions. The Great Hall was noisy with talking and laughter as the guests formed groups around individual tables to begin a night of games. The lighting and atmosphere made Faye feel like anything could happen.

Faye loved card parties, especially ones hosted by Clive, as he always brought the fun. She was especially honored to be invited to this one, as it would be a private gathering, including Duke Hartwell and his older sister, Lady Mariah Jarvis. The Jarvis family was closely acquainted with the Fitzpatricks, and so on occasion, Faye found herself in their company.

Faye's friendly fondness for Clive, now Lord Spalding, had turned into an attraction. They had maintained their close friendship, but that was a double-edged sword, for she was afraid they may always remain only friends. She deeply appreciated that unique and special relationship, for Clive, while popular, cultivated few close acquaintances. But it wasn't wholly satisfying anymore.

"Are you ready to lose, Spalding?" Faye challenged as he dealt the cards.

"Are you?" he countered.

"History is on my side. When was the last time you won?" she teased.

"I have a different partner tonight."

Faye snorted. "I've played with your brother, and he's decent. No, I believe your losing streak is your special power." *Perhaps that's not the best way to persuade him towards me.*

"Where is that quiet, handsome one?" Daisy asked off-handedly.

"Probably shooting something," Clive muttered.

Daisy let out a peal of laughter. "He's not that bad. Though it lends him a certain aura of manly mystery, don't you think, Faye?"

Faye laid down a card. "I think you've read too many novels."

"At least someone here is thinking straight," said Clive.

"He's like a silent wild man but a gentleman," Daisy continued. "Such an intriguing combination. Gives me shivers. No telling what's boiling under that cool demeanor—"

"Thank you, Miss Caldwell, but I think we've explored that topic enough," Clive cut in.

Daisy raised an eyebrow. "Feeling a mite threatened, Spalding? You're not without your own aura."

"You may discuss that at great length if you wish."

The girls laughed, and they continued their card game.

Faye glanced at Geoff, who'd just re-entered the room and stood close to the door, his more serious countenance contrasting with the freer atmosphere surrounding him. Intriguing was a good word to describe him, for he did arrest attention at first sight but then slowly disappeared. Geoff wasn't dull; he just wasn't as lively and outgoing as his older brother, who usually commanded a room.

"Any other intrigues for us this summer, Spalding?" Faye asked as she directed attention back to her hand and laid down a card.

"I'm now a businessman," Clive answered with mock seriousness. "I must leave my wild ways behind."

Daisy snorted.

"If my business happens to take me to a tropical island that absolutely demands I partake of its diversions, I can't help that." Clive's eyes twinkled. "But I can't get too wild with Fitz. You know how formal he can be."

Daisy rolled her eyes. "You make your brother sound like an old man."

"If I didn't know better, I'd think you have a fancy for him, Daisy," Faye remarked.

"No, that's far too deep; it's only a shallow fascination. But his eyes have not left this table since he came back into the room."

"Maybe he wants to play?" Faye ventured.

"He's just being odd," Clive muttered. "I wish he'd stop doing those sorts of things. He needs to loosen up."

"Geoff is fine," Faye said. "It's no good for everyone to be as gregarious as you are."

"Maybe you'd prefer him to play instead of me."

"Of course not." Faye gave him a mischievous grin. "I enjoy winning too much."

Clive smiled back. "Then we'll have to play together the whole evening if it gives you that much pleasure."

"I'm very happy to hear that," Faye replied. *Maybe I'm finally getting on with him.*

*****

Geoff

Geoff enjoyed card parties as they were a perfect way to be sociable without socializing excessively. He could be around people and not talk too much.

Geoff preferred Yardley, but Spalding held its own mystique as the original earldom for the Fitzpatrick family. Several generations later, they had been given a marquisette and Yardley, so the families since have established it as their principal residence. It had become customary for the oldest son to assume Spalding when he turned twenty-one until he inherited. Clive, being Clive, had given the place a more party-like atmosphere.

Towards the end of the night, Geoff grew weary of company and annoyed that Faye had spent the entire night with Clive and seemed to have a grand time doing so. He thought of joining them a couple of times, but Clive grabbed another partner before Geoff could get over there. He made himself comfortable on the couch in front of the fireplace with a drink. The great hall was well lit, but night had fallen, so the section was darker and only illuminated by the flames of the fire. It was a peaceful reprieve.

Mariah took a seat next to him. "How are you, Geoff?"

"I'm well, especially with this glass of wine."

She laughed.

He'd known Mariah since they were children and had always liked her, for she understood him. She was currently twenty-seven years of age, unmarried, and had remained at Hartwell with her father. The Jarvis siblings bore a strong resemblance to one another and had hickory-colored eyes and loosely curled dark hair.

Geoff sobered. "I should be the one asking you. Things could not have been easy these last few months."

Mariah sighed. "You're right. We have an excellent steward and land agent, but father did not leave affairs very well. And you know how Richard is..." she trailed off.

All over the place and tightly wound.

"And he's doing this mill and loom thing," Mariah continued. "I'm afraid he'll burn himself out."

Geoff didn't wish to get involved, but he wanted to help his friends. "Let me know if you need assistance. I'd be happy to render aid."

"Thank you. That's very kind."

The two sat quietly.

"She'll come around," Mariah said.

Geoff stilled. "What do you mean?"

"Miss Faye. She'll come around."

Geoff downed the rest of his drink.

"Another?" Mariah asked wryly.

"Please."

Mariah had another brought for him.

"Am I that obvious?" Geoff muttered. *First Aunt Bonnie and now Mariah...*

She chuckled. "No, especially not tonight. But I thought I detected a partiality on your part the last time we visited Yardley."

Geoff exhaled.

"You may need to fight for her. I suspect you haven't really done that."

"It's not like I'm not around."

"Yes, like the rug on the floor that you let Clive walk upon."

Geoff looked at her sharply.

"The three of you are quite entertaining to watch," Mariah remarked. "I like Miss Faye a great deal, but I believe she, in a manner of speaking, likes bright, shiny things. Not that I'm saying you should change yourself, for your quietness has its own appeal, but you may need to be more demonstrative. Despite her fine qualities, Miss Faye is not a mind reader."

"She prefers Clive."

"Make sure she knows she has another option," Mariah said pointedly. "It probably won't take much. It's not as though she doesn't have a high regard for you; it just seems she's never seen you in that light. And to be fair, I can't entirely blame her."

"I'm not suitor material?" Geoff asked dryly.

"You don't seem interested in it."

He supposed he didn't do the things most young men do to indicate they want to court. *Mariah may have a point.* "You could have a conversation with Clive about him opening his eyes."

"I could, but I think you and Faye are the better pair — enough commonalities to be compatible and differences to balance each other out. I have the feeling Clive and Faye are too similar. And Clive needs some help."

Geoff laughed.

"He's a mess like Richard," Mariah remarked. "It's a wonder the two of them haven't gone over a cliff together yet."

"Self-preservation is strong," said Geoff, still chuckling. "I think they have enough sense to surround themselves with people who will check them."

"Yes, people like you. You're a good brother. Keep looking after him, even if it gets hard."

It's getting very hard.

As they were getting their things before leaving, Clive nudged Geoff. "I saw you talking to Mariah. She'd be good for you."

"There's nothing of that sort happening."

Clive wiggled his eyebrows and then walked off.

Objectively, Clive was right. Mariah was a great woman.

But she wasn't Faye.

CHAPTER 6

The Commission

Geoff

GEOFF AND CLIVE STOOD on the Armstrong's porch. Oakes Hollow was an old and impressive estate, and Father was pleased Mr. Armstrong was hospitable and allowed many visitors to tour the grounds annually. Mr. Armstrong's parents and older brother hadn't been so inclined. Presently, the home was filled with lots of good cheer, which Geoff greatly admired.

Not that his own home was an unhappy one. His parents were very fond of one another. Father was kind and Mother attentive to the boys. While Geoff liked the peace and quiet of Yardley, he also enjoyed the unabashed display of warmth and activity amongst the Armstrongs. He could attest to his own difficulties being expressive in that manner. There's a vulnerability in declaring himself such to others, and Geoff found safety in his protective shell.

The Fitzpatrick brothers were shown into the drawing room, where Geoff took in the magnificent view out the porch doors. Generations of careful attention yielded garden showcases of which the family could be proud. He liked many things about Oakes Hollow's gardens, but his favorite feature could be seen here — four glorious hornbeam trees that superbly framed the fountain and lawn. Yardley had attractive ones too, but these were wonderfully whimsical, as though they expressed their personalities in the way they twisted and turned, their green leaves lighter in color than the norm, scattering sunlight across the water in the pond. The scene would make a fabulous landscape composition.

Geoff grinned as the whole Armstrong family descended upon them. Everyone took seats, and Clive stated the purpose of their call.

"Could you please have those delicious little apple tarts—" Miss Daisy began.

"Daisy!" Mrs. Caldwell exclaimed. "Where are your manners?"

"He asked, and no one has apple tarts like the Fitzpatricks."

"Just because Lords Yardley and Spalding inquired after our wants don't mean we need to express them so freely."

"But that's exactly what Father wishes," Clive assured them. "I wouldn't mind some apple tart myself. Excellent suggestion."

"Splendid, Clive!" Faye exclaimed.

"Lord Spalding, please inform your father we're all looking forward to the dinner with great anticipation," Mr. Armstrong said. "He always exceeds our expectations."

"He'll be glad to hear that." Clive turned towards Faye. "How is the sculpture of your grandfather progressing?"

"Fairly well. I may need to arrange a visit to do additional studies of him."

"I've never met your grandfather but have heard much about him from your father," Clive said.

"Would you like to see him?" Faye chuckled. "His partially done sculpture, that is?"

"I'd be delighted!" Clive jumped up and started across the room, following Faye.

"Mr. Fitzpatrick, since you enjoy art, perhaps you'd enjoy seeing the piece as well," said Mr. Armstrong.

"Yes, of course!" exclaimed Faye. "I want you to come too, Geoff."

As the brothers walked with Faye down the hall, she spoke with Clive, her smile bright and remarks witty.

Geoff checked his jealousy. *I should be used to this by now.*

They followed Faye into the room where she sculpted. Geoff blinked at the brightness — the white walls and sheets complimented the natural light. Tall windows allowed a perfect view of the gazebo and another pond surrounded by colossal terracotta pots. It was an ideal space for artistry, but also a remarkable area in general and an indication of how much Mr. Armstrong valued and encouraged Faye's sculpting.

Geoff was acquainted with few who so steadily followed through on their plans and was pleased she'd accomplished her goal. Faye reached out and boldly seized what she wanted.

I wish I had a goal. It's little wonder I don't interest her. Clive seems to always have a plan afoot.

Clive monopolized Faye's attention, like he always did.

Faye was more than happy to give it to him, like she always was.

Geoff grew more and more annoyed, as usual.

But today, he'd reached a boiling point. *I'm tired of being obscured by Clive.* "Would you sculpt a likeness of me?" Geoff asked Faye.

The other two grew silent and stared at him.

"I'm willing to pay any price you name," Geoff continued.

"You want me to do a bust of you?" Faye repeated incredulously.

Geoff nodded. "I'm surprised that seems so extraordinary."

"It's such an honor," she practically whispered. "Your family could commission real artists to do likenesses of you."

Geoff raised an eyebrow. "Are you not a real artist, Faye?"

She flushed and squared her shoulders. "Yes, you're absolutely right." Faye clapped her hands, beaming at him now. "Thank you so much!" she exclaimed. "What a great compliment!"

*****

Faye

Faye almost pinched herself. *I've received a request to do the bust of the son of a marquess. Geoff will be a wonderful subject to sculpt.* But if one of the Fitzpatrick brothers were to ask, she was surprised it was Geoff since she was closer to Clive. She studied Geoff as he looked at an unfinished bird figurine on a table.

He suddenly glanced up and held her gaze.

Feeling conscious, Faye cast her eyes downward. When she raised them again, Geoff had turned his attention to another uncompleted work.

She cleared her throat. "I promise I'll actually finish your piece."

He chuckled. "I never doubted you would. Do you usually leave your projects unfinished?"

"That seems to be the pattern into which I've fallen. Apparently, I lack a steadiness in purpose."

"I think not," Geoff replied. "Perhaps you only require a stronger motivation."

"But I enjoy sculpting," Faye said.

"Of course, but I'm sure you seek significance to your activities, even in the pursuits you enjoy. I believe you'd be dissatisfied with a life of endless merriments and pleasures."

"Yes, absolutely."

Clive smirked. "Faye, dear, I know you enjoy your pleasures. That's why we get on so well."

She frowned. That comment made her sound hedonistic, and she didn't want to appear so to Geoff. "We do, but it's not all I want out of life, Clive."

It suddenly struck her that as long as she'd been friends with Geoff, she didn't know him well. "What do you seek?" she asked him.

Geoff seemed to study her again, his penetrating eyes making her feel conscious once more. Like he could really see her. She wasn't entirely sure she was comfortable with what he might discover.

But this time, she held his gaze. *Let him find out. Better for him to know the truth.*

"Unlike yourself, I've not found a worthwhile occupation yet," he replied.

Clive snorted. "I gave you an opportunity, and you shoved it away."

"I clearly outlined my reservations, and you didn't address them."

"What was the opportunity?" Faye asked.

Clive briefly described what T.H.E.T.A. was and his own shipping venture.

"It sounds exciting, but Geoff always struck me as an artistic being," Faye said.

Clive smirked. "Yes, the moody, emotional man."

Geoff glared at him.

"No, it just seems to me his interests lie elsewhere," Faye clarified, tugging on a curl. "I could understand why he'd decline, though he may be an asset to your outfit."

Geoff raised an eyebrow. "How so?"

"It sounds as though the operation could use a bit of structure."

"My words exactly," Geoff said.

"I think you could provide that and give things solidity and strength," Faye finished.

"Things are strong," Clive insisted.

Geoff appeared deep in thought as he turned the bird figurine in his hands. He blitzed her with a smile. "I believe I'd rather become a patron of the arts."

Faye grinned back. "I think that would suit you perfectly."

CHAPTER 7

Opportunities or Disasters?

Geoff

"YOU AVOIDED THE SUBJECT before, but now you can't escape, especially after all that rubbish you told Faye." Clive called as he slowed his horse to a walk.

They were returning from calling on the Armstrongs, and Clive planned on remaining for dinner and staying the night.

Geoff scowled as he stopped his horse so Clive could catch up. "To what rubbish are you referring? If I recall, my comments were few and accurate. You did most of the talking on that topic."

"A patron of the arts? If you're helping people, why don't you start with your friends."

"I'm helping Faye." Geoff's horse began walking to match Clive's pace.

Clive gave him a look.

Geoff sighed. "Jarvis is taking on too much?"

"I think it'd be better for a man like you to do the Derbyshire project, leaving Richard to work with Thurston."

"I know little about running textile mills."

"There are enough people involved who know how to run the mills. It'd be more about coordinating, organizing, and overseeing the modifications taking place. I'm afraid Richard won't execute the changes properly, and then Lord Vaughnryd will pull out. He had to be talked into doing this in the first place."

"Why did he agree?"

"Lord Thurston and Richard offered to take over his operations entirely so he could concentrate on his quarries, building materials, and coal. That interested him more than the mill expansion."

"You'd still have to address his core inducement since I can't run mills."

"Your involvement would buy us time, and I think you and he would be a better fit than he and Richard," Clive explained. "Lord Vaughnryd is more cautious by nature and was perfectly happy just providing for him and his. I think you'd work well with those wishes."

Geoff took his horse around a large rock as he contemplated the situation. If he were to be involved, he'd much rather work with a less ambitious subset than the whole menagerie Jarvis was juggling.

"I'm asking you to act as a buffer," Clive continued. "Tie up the loose ends Richard leaves behind and fill in the blanks. He appears all over the place, but in truth, he craves order, and it's usually there amongst the seeming chaos. If he's doing too much, there's only so much he can humanly attend to, and I have my own shipping interests to tend to." He gave a happy exhale. "I can't wait for my chocolate."

Geoff groaned as he joined Clive's side again. *Another person who doesn't always fill in the blanks. He better hope no one steals his goods off the ships.*

"Race you," Clive challenged.

Geoff grinned. They usually did this here. Leaving the path and crossing the expansive grassland was an enjoyable shortcut to Yardley, which was just beyond the hill where the grassland ended. "One day you'll get tired of losing," Geoff joked.

Clive chuckled and took off with Geoff fast behind him.

Geoff slowed his horse as he raced through the gates towards the stables. This wasn't a small enterprise, and if something went wrong, it could go very wrong. But Geoff supposed Clive was trying to prevent that by involving him, and he couldn't fault his brother for that.

"I'd like to speak with Lord Vaughnryd and Jarvis before committing to anything," Geoff said to Clive when he rode in. Geoff dismounted.

"That sounds good."

I hope Clive isn't pulling me into a catastrophe already in the making.

*****

Faye

Aunt Bonnie poked her head into the sculpture room late the next morning. "Do you have a moment? I have news I believe you'll want to hear."

Faye wiped her hands on her apron. "I love news, and I have some of my own to share."

She should help with the ball preparations anyway, not sculpt. Excitement was mounting for the big night tomorrow. Faye joined everyone in the morning room.

"Lady Girnwood and her daughter are seeking a traveling companion to accompany them on a tour of Scotland," Aunt Bonnie announced.

Faye gasped. She was recently of the mind that a travel adventure, like a European tour, would develop her sculpting and drawing both in skill and subject matter. Geoff's words about her seeking significance through her art was an insightful comment as she'd told no one why doing Grandfather Sabo's bust filled her with so much delight. Scotland wasn't a European tour, but it'd be a nice start.

However, she didn't care for the Gillinghams. She'd always felt they considered her beneath them, though their manner seemed to displease many.

"The expression on your face, Faye," Daisey remarked. "We should leave the Gillinghams out of it, and you and I can embark on our own Scotland tour. It'd be much lovelier."

"Absolutely not," said Aunt Chelsea. "No telling what kind of craziness you'd get Faye into."

"But if you seriously wish to do that sort of trip, I can make inquiries," Papa offered.

The girls grinned at one another.

"It would be terribly expensive, Wyatt," remarked Aunt Chelsea.

"To do properly, yes. But I think it might be worth the experience. I'll check into it."

Daisy squealed.

"Wyatt, you spoil them something terrible," Aunt Bonnie said.

"Making up for all the trouble I caused everyone as a young man."

"I'll still pursue the trip with the Gillinghams," Faye said. "It would be a convenient opportunity."

Daisy snorted. "Convenience sometimes comes at a heavy price."

"Be careful, Daisy dear. You actually made a sensible comment," teased Aunt Chelsea.

"I must keep you all on your toes with the unexpected."

Faye told them about Geoff's commission.

Papa nodded approvingly. "If you do this and the bust of your grandfather, that might get you some notice, Faye."

Her father left the room to tend to correspondence, and the Caldwells departed to purchase last-minute items for the ball.

Aunt Bonnie gave Faye an appraising look when everyone was gone. "Have you ever wondered if Mr. Geoffrey is sweet on you?"

Faye stared at her.

"I suppose not." Aunt Bonnie laughed. "You look as though I told you the cow jumped over the moon."

"That would be more believable. The idea had never occurred to me, and I'm sure he is not."

Geoff sweet on me? I'm nothing more than a playmate or companion, and now someone commissioned to do his bust.

"He's not the gentleman with whom you're marooned on friend island?" Aunt Bonnie's eyes shone with mirth.

"Geoff and I are close companions, but he'd never seek a romantic attachment with me."

"And what about you of him?" Aunt Bonnie asked.

Faye fidgeted. "Geoff is so serious and quiet. We'd never work."

"Indeed." The smile remained on her aunt's face.

The idea is preposterous. Clive is a much better match for me.

CHAPTER 8

Court Me

Faye

GUESTS MINGLED in the downstairs foyer and on the balcony as they arrived for The Oakes Hollow Ball. The area was festively decorated, and the adjoining secondary drawing and music rooms were filled with refreshments and additional seating.

Faye was with her father in the foyer receiving guests, so by the time she entered the ballroom upstairs, the evening was in full swing, and the first dance was coming to a close. She had hoped tonight would yield her the opportunity to incline Clive's interest in a different direction, and she made her way towards him across the room.

"Perusing, Lord Spalding?" she asked dryly.

He turned and grinned. "There are many eligible dance partners to choose from. You look very well tonight. Who will you choose, Miss Faye?"

"I'd dance with you if you'd ask me."

"Certainly. I'll make sure to ask at some point this evening."

Faye tried not to frown. She never doubted Clive considered her one of his closest companions, but she'd like to be viewed as special, not like he'll tend to her when he got around to it. "I'm a touch old to be choosing partners anyway," she remarked, shrugging off her annoyance. "In a couple of years, I'll be deemed an old maid and unmarriageable."

"Twenty-three isn't too old at all. Some say it's the perfect age for a man to choose as his wife."

"From where did you hear that?"

"Book reading."

"You did some of that instead of gallivanting?"

Clive smirked. "Marriage is a most important endeavor, and I decided I should be well-learned on the subject."

Faye shook her head.

"You're just too particular," Clive remarked. "I can sympathize with that. I'm selective myself."

Faye stifled a sigh. *I just chose the wrong man, and his gray eyes are ogling the other ladies.*

Clive rubbed his hands together. "I think I'll start high and work my way down."

Faye snorted. "Don't let me keep you from your first victim."

Clive laughed and then walked away. He and the lady in question would make a charming couple.

"You appear as though you swallowed something sour, Miss Faye." Geoff walked up beside her.

"I apologize, for that must be an ugly face to behold."

"On the contrary." He paused. "May I have a dance?"

Faye widened her eyes. Unlike his brother, Geoff rarely danced. "I'd be delighted."

"How about this one?" He held out an arm.

Faye grinned as she took it. *That was the response I'd hoped for from Clive.*

Geoff led her to the floor, also looking very well. He was never a flashy dresser in the latest styles, but tonight, his appearance was one of simplistic affluence in hues that excellently complemented his natural coloring.

After a few minutes, Faye exclaimed, "You're the best dancer out here!"

"Mother made sure we were well taught."

He had an ease and smoothness to his movements that most young gentlemen lacked. Geoff apparently took to the lessons better than Clive, for his brother didn't dance as well, though he was a diverting partner.

"Would you be so kind as to favor me with another one?" Geoff asked when the music ceased. "So we could get a full dance in."

"Absolutely. That was short, and I'd love to dance with such an able partner. Your secret is out."

*****

Geoff led Faye off the floor towards the windows when their second dance ended.

"Thank you," said Faye. "That was quite enjoyable."

Geoff chuckled. "Do I detect a hint of shock in your voice?"

Faye felt flushed. "What was I supposed to imagine? You never dance."

"True." He gazed outside, still holding her arm.

"Would you rather be out there?" she teased.

"I would actually." He glanced at her, green eyes intense. "Would you take a turn with me?"

"Outside?" Father had the premises around the fountain well lit for special events like the ball, so that wasn't an issue, but it was still a curious request.

Geoff winced and then released her arm. "Forgive me. I'm sure you wish to engage another dance partner. Thank you for doing me the honor."

Though it was unusual to focus so much attention on one partner unless there was an understanding, Faye was enjoying his company. "You give me too much credit, and it would be good to get a little fresh air. If you'll excuse me while I get a shawl."

"Of course. I'll wait by the stairs."

Five minutes later, they were ambling past the flowers towards the fountain lit by a series of lanterns and a full moon. The air was warm and slightly humid, but not unpleasantly so.

Geoff seemed preoccupied though more relaxed than when they were indoors. They walked around the half-circle of the pond and then down the path towards the archway and stairs leading to another section of the gardens. Faye was about to ask where he planned on wandering when he released her arm and headed towards a hornbeam tree.

Faye grimaced. *The grass might stain my new shoes.* But she was just far enough that a conversation would be awkward, so she followed him to the tree.

Except for the water trickling from the fountain, it was quiet outside; sounds of the ball had faded behind them. Geoff studied her for a moment as he leaned against the tree, the shadows making his already defined features appear sharper.

Faye swallowed and began fidgeting. "Yes?"

"What is it about Clive that has you so enraptured?" he asked softly.

Faye gaped at him. Geoff tended to be a direct speaker, probably to cut down on the length of time he must talk. But she was unaccustomed to fielding personal questions of a romantic nature from him. Or from any gentleman for that matter.

She crossed her arms. "Who says I'm enraptured?"

"I don't understand why you're wasting your time with him."

No use playing the fool with Geoff. He's known me too long. "I wondered that myself tonight," she muttered, dropping her arms.

Geoff chuckled. "What is it about him?"

"We've been friends for years and are usually of the same mind."

"I can understand that, but if he's too much of a knock-head to see you, don't you think it's time to move on?" Geoff paused. "You're a beautiful woman, Faye. You shouldn't have to convince a man to look at you."

Faye's stomach somersaulted. She might be wholly infatuated with Clive, but she wasn't immune to being called beautiful by a good-looking man like Geoff.

"You could teach him a lesson." He gave her a sly smile. "I think you should court me."

"Court you?"

He straightened and took a step away from the tree. "I suppose I thought very wrong."

Faye cringed. "I'm sorry, Geoff; I didn't intend for my words to come out in that manner." He was the last person she'd want to hurt. "It's just such an extraordinary idea from you. Why do you want to do it?"

"It can't be because I like you?"

Faye gave him a look.

"It can't be because one reason is I like you?"

Faye raised an eyebrow.

"It drives me wild that he looks over you and panders to other women," Geoff said. "He should have whisked you off long ago."

Of course, the wrong brother comprehends this. "I still don't understand why you want to do this."

"I just told you."

"Geoff—"

He sighed. "Can't one friend do another a favor? And it's even better that I can stick one to Clive at the same time."

Faye regarded him for a second. "I didn't realize you ever wanted to stick it to Clive. I feel like you're changing right before my eyes tonight."

"Not changing, just perhaps displaying a different side." He paused. "Do you like what you're seeing?"

"I don't know," Faye answered, perplexed. "Why do you think this scheme will make a difference to him? As you pointed out, he looks over me in that way as it is."

"Trust me. Clive will notice, and he'll care. He's taking you for granted, and once that's threatened by me, of all people, you'll have his undivided attention."

Faye studied him again.

"Am I that unappealing?" Geoff gave her a small smile.

Faye could tell he tried to make the question light, but she sensed a tiny bit of hurt underneath.

"It's not that." Faye paused. *Wait, it's not that?* "I'm just surprised, is all."

Why am I still pining over Clive? I've been in front of his person for years. Geoff is well-favored, intelligent, and we've been friends just as long.

And Geoff asked to court me.

Faye held her chin up. "Yes, Geoff. I accept."

He gave her a crooked grin. "You chose wisely."

"It might be hard to pull this off since I do care for another, even if I shouldn't."

"I'll have to work harder to convince you otherwise."

Faye's jaw dropped. *He might not have to work too hard. This is definitely not a side I've ever seen of Geoff.*

*****

Clive intercepted Faye at the drink table after returning from her walk with Geoff. "Did Geoff lose a wager with you?"

"Is that the only way I can get a gentleman to dance with me?"

He rolled his eyes. "Of course not; it's just Geoff never dances."

"He also never courts, but he asked me to do that as well."

"I beg your pardon?"

"We're courting."

"Why would Geoff court you?" Faye glared at him.

He winced. "I didn't mean it like that. I just pictured you with someone different, definitely not my younger brother. Isn't that breaking the rules?"

"What rules?"

"Isn't courting your closest friend's brother improper decorum or something?"

He must have lost his senses. "It occurs frequently. What planet are you living on?"

"I thought Earth, but I'm not sure anymore."

Faye walked away from him.

Clive chased after her. "You're truly courting Geoff?"

"Yes. This shouldn't be so unbelievable. From a mercenary suitor standpoint, he's a great catch, and from a human being standpoint, he's infinitely better." Faye gave a sigh of disgust and walked away again.

"Why are you mad at me?" Clive pleaded, running after her again.

Faye stopped short. "You truly have no idea, do you?"

It killed her to ask that. Without waiting for a reply, she left the ballroom and went to the fountain, giving her cheek an angry swipe.

Clive doesn't see me at all.

She set her jaw. *I'll show him. By the time I'm through, he'll beg to court me.*

She marched back into the ballroom and searched for Geoff.

Perfect. He's speaking with Papa.

She strode across the floor and slipped her arm through his.

Geoff smiled at her.

"Papa, did Geoff tell you we're courting?" Faye asked.

✵✵✵✵✵

Geoff

"What game are you playing?" Clive snapped at Geoff fifteen minutes later as he stood by a table laden with custards.

"What are you talking about?" Geoff asked mildly.

"What do you mean by courting Faye?"

"You mean why would I want to court the intelligent, well-off, gorgeous, gentleman's daughter who happens to have wit, knows how to have fun, and can sculpt a bust of me? You're right, Clive; what was I thinking?"

Clive's face turned red. "What has gotten into you?"

"I finally decide to be something other than a wallflower, and you take issue with it?"

"You've never been interested in Faye before."

"You don't know that, and neither have you."

"Faye has always been my closest friend."

"And she can stay your friend while she becomes my wife."

Something dangerous flashed in Clive's eyes.

Geoff didn't know what had gotten into him. He was acting outside himself right now.

"If you do anything to hurt her—"

"Right back at you," Geoff spat out. "You're the one who's been hurting her, and I'm tired of standing by and watching it."

"The Fitzpatrick boys," called Lady Helena behind them.

Geoff tried not to make a face as they turned. She was the last person he wanted to interact with right now.

Clive's smile looked hard to wear. "At your service. What can we do for you, Lady Helena?"

"I was hoping to have a chance to visit with you. It's so hard to tear the two of you away from Miss Faye. I suppose she's pretty. In a way."

Geoff set his jaw.

"Did I say something amiss?" she asked.

"Miss Faye has been a close friend of ours for years," Clive answered rather coolly. "We naturally gravitate towards one another at gatherings such as these."

"It's kind of you to pay her such attentions, though one would wonder if it weren't more than that."

"They won't have to wonder for long as, apparently, my brother has just begun a courtship with her," Clive said.

"Indeed? I'm quite surprised. The son of a marquess with..." She made an odd motion with her hand. "I'd think you'd have chosen differently."

Geoff was about to deliver a retort when her mother, Lady Girnwood, joined her side. "Just the young men I was seeking. I hoped to engage one of you for a dance with my dear Helena. You know she's new in the neighborhood and quite shy about asking."

"Mother," Lady Helena said with false embarrassment.

"At first, I thought Lord Spalding would be my only option," Lady Girnwood continued. "But I just witnessed how splendidly you dance, Mr. Fitzpatrick. The other ladies had positively assured me you never take a turn. What a big secret you've been hiding."

I absolutely cannot dance with Lady Helena right now. "If you'll excuse me, Lady Girnwood. I have a sudden, severe headache I must tend to."

"Of course, Mr. Fitzpatrick," she replied. "I hope it's not serious."

"It's nothing a little quiet won't ease." Geoff gave them a short bow and then strode away.

Usually, the Gillinghams didn't vex him so, but Clive had worked him to a state where he could hardly think, and they made it worse.

He returned to the hornbeam, leaning against the trunk and taking a deep breath as he listened to the water in the fountain. *That's better. Faye agreed to court me at this spot just an hour before.*

He grinned.

Geoff sincerely wanted to court Faye, and he was proud that he'd taken the plunge and finally asked. He'd overheard her conversation with Clive, when he had essentially brushed her off, like she was of little matter. Ordinary. Geoff had to set that right. But he shouldn't have dragged Faye into his complexities with Clive, for as much as he liked Faye, his rivalry with his brother was motivation too.

She may not like me yet, but Faye finally sees me. She deserves better, and I can give it to her.

CHAPTER 9

True Motivations

Faye

A WEEK LATER, the Armstrongs arrived at Yardley for the Fitzpatrick dinner and were shown into the drawing room where Lord and Lady Yardley were already waiting.

"Faye!" Lady Yardley exclaimed and took her arm, guiding her to a seat by the window.

Faye was surprised. She spoke with Lady Yardley regularly when she accompanied Aunt Bonnie to call, but it was unusual for the marchioness to single her out in this manner.

"I'm pleased to hear Geoff requested to court you," Lady Yardley said after they sat down.

Faye put on a bright smile. "I'm happy you're pleased. I was quite astonished when he asked."

"Were you? I wasn't." Lady Yardley winked. "Enjoy yourself, my dear." She walked over to Faye's aunts.

Daisy took her place. "Did she give her blessing or threaten you?"

"It wasn't quite a blessing, but she was pleased."

"Very good. You've done well for yourself."

Geoff and Clive entered the room.

"If you'll excuse me, Daisy." Faye rose.

Daisy yanked her back down. "You're hopeless. Don't be so eager. Let him come to you."

"But I really must speak with him."

Daisy snorted. "Of course you must. Be still. You have all evening."

Faye caught Geoff's eye from across the room and made a slight motion with her hand.

He walked towards her.

"Most impressive," Daisy whispered. "It's even better that he comes at your slightest command."

Faye shook her head.

Geoff bowed before Daisy. "Good evening, Miss Daisy."

"I know it's a good evening for you, Mr. Fitzpatrick." She gave him a sly smile.

He chuckled and then excused himself and Faye. "What's wrong?" he asked in a lowered tone as they walked away.

"How do you know something is wrong?" *Daisy hadn't even guessed that.*

"It's all over your face, and your come-hither wasn't really flirtatious."

"You know my facial expressions that well?" Faye asked, astonished.

"I've known you for years. Yes, I know your facial expressions."

"Oh." Faye mulled that over. *Do I know his?* "I didn't mean to be so authoritative."

"You needn't apologize. It's an indication there's a problem."

"Your mother is pleased we're courting."

Geoff appeared amused. "That's the big problem?"

"It will be if she discovers it's not real."

His face went blank. "It's not as though we loathe one another."

"I know, and we probably have better regard for each other than some courting couples. But she'd be disappointed with our true motivations."

"Those might not be as clear as you believe they are."

Faye stared at him. *He's choosing now to speak in riddles?*

"You can back out if you wish." Geoff paused. "But the Gillinghams will be here tonight, and I suspect Lady Helena has her sights set on Clive."

That's a new development. "I'm not surprised. How likely is he to return the attention?"

"Your guess is as good as mine. I don't believe he actually likes her, but as the marquess incumbent, he could talk himself into a match if he believes it'll be advantageous."

Faye bit her lip. "I suppose a match with Lady Helena would be better than one with me."

"I think the obvious choice is you. You might not have the rank, but you have more land and money, and in terms of personality and talent, there's just no comparison."

"That's kind of you to say."

Geoff exhaled, looking frustrated.

"What's wrong?" Faye asked.

"It's nothing." He paused. "I'll be away for a little while."

"So soon after we began courting?" Faye teased him. "Is this foreshadowing what married life will be like?"

Geoff turned pink. "No, of course not. I'd imagine you'd have to pry me away from you."

"Nice line. Good idea. We should practice."

Geoff gave her a look.

"You realize our plan would work better if Clive actually sees us together instead of you running away from me." Faye chuckled.

"I'm doing this in part because of your observations. That should get you a gold star," Geoff remarked dryly.

"Excellent. So this is for that T.H.E.T.A. thing you two spoke of?"

Geoff nodded and told her a bit about what he planned to accomplish during his trip.

"I'm surprised you're so reticent about this," Faye said.

"It doesn't happen often, but things can blow up with Jarvis. And he's usually not the one held responsible when it does."

"Were you on the receiving end?"

"No, but others have been, especially when we were boys at school."

"I have every confidence you'll prevent things from falling to pieces."

Geoff peered at her. "Truly?"

"Absolutely."

"Thank you." Geoff beamed. "That means much to me."

Faye smiled back. *What a lovely grin he has. It's like sunshine.*

"I think we've appeared the part of besotted suitors long enough for now," Geoff said. "Shall we join the others? Be a happy party before the Gilling-hams arrive?"

Faye took his arm again. "Certainly."

*****

Geoff

Geoff's conversation with Faye unsettled him. Faye was right about Mama; if she discovered what was going on between him and Clive regarding Faye, she'd be angry with both of them.

Faye still had no inkling about his true feelings for her and apparently perceived his hints at the ball as jokes. Perhaps, it would be best to speak plainly, but then she'd probably think him absurd. He felt uneasy that he'd essentially manipulated her into staying in a courtship with him when she clearly had misgivings.

"Lady Girnwood, I heard you and your daughter are to take a tour of Scotland in the near future," Mrs. Caldwell remarked during dinner.

Lady Girnwood nodded. "Helena's father had set aside a fund so she could do so, and we decided to try this year."

"Our Faye was also hoping to expand her horizons," said Mrs. Caldwell.

"Was she?" Lady Girnwood asked off-handedly. "We received many expressions of interest, and we're very particular in making sure a young lady of the highest caliber accompanies us."

Geoff frowned. "I can assure you Miss Faye is of the highest caliber, and her attendance would elevate your experience."

Faye flushed.

Lady Girnwood chuckled. "It's only natural Miss Faye's suitor would speak of her with such flattery, and it's very kind of you to do so, Mr. Fitzpatrick."

"It wasn't flattery," Geoff replied. "I only spoke the facts as they currently stand."

"We'd be happy to consider Miss Faye if she wishes. I was merely saying we'll scrutinize all candidates to ensure the best experience for everyone."

His father cleared his throat. "Absolutely, Lady Girnwood. That sounds very reasonable, and I wish you success." He changed the subject.

*****

"I think I liked you better silent," Clive muttered as the men made their way to the library after dinner.

"I don't understand how you could listen as Lady Girnwood attacked your so-called closest friend without saying a word," Geoff retorted.

Clive rolled his eyes. "We get it. You must ardently defend your woman. Just soften your tone. Dowager Lady Girnwood and her daughter are without a husband and father. You don't want to come across as a bully."

Geoff didn't believe he had, but he was curt, and the Gillinghams lacking familial protection had merit. "How precarious is their situation? I thought Lady Helena's uncle was looking after them."

"At present, he is, though that could change if he married. If he had not, their circumstances would have been reduced. Their family didn't blend well like the Armstrongs did, so it's still not an ideal situation."

"I'll apologize later."

"I don't think there's cause for that; just watch yourself before you say or do something you regret."

CHAPTER 10

T.H.E.T.A.

Geoff

GEOFF LEFT FOR HARTWELL the day after the dinner. It was less complicated to meet with Jarvis, as he was only an hour's drive from Yardley, and neither one of them had families to juggle.

Hartwell was a massive estate that looked careworn. Jarvis would be a good man to turn that around, but it would take time. Previously, he had charge of another property, but Hartwell was the family's primary residence and much larger.

The two men exchanged warm hellos, and then Geoff suggested they take a walk since he could stand to stretch his legs, and Jarvis appeared a bit antsy.

"What are your plans for the estate?" Geoff asked as he glanced at some rather sad looking shrubbery.

Jarvis exhaled. "I hardly know where to begin."

"It's not as though the place is a complete shambles. Mariah mentioned you have excellent men working with you."

"I do, but I'm tired of the chaos." He kicked at a pebble. "That was one advantage of hiding at my old place."

"Then it's a wonder you did this T.H.E.T.A. venture," Geoff said carefully. "It seems put together chaotically."

"Innovations like that loom will encourage efficient production and create a high-quality product. It's perfect. If I'd known a year or two ago I'd be a duke, I probably wouldn't have started, but it's done now, and I think it's for the best. I'll see it through somehow."

"Would my services be useful?" Geoff offered, still wary, though it sounded like Jarvis wasn't any happier with the patchwork than he was.

Jarvis stopped walking. "In what capacity?"

"Clive thought assistance from an organizational and communications standpoint might be useful. The expansion of two mills at the same time will be difficult to oversee on your own."

"It will be. Could you oversee the Vaughnryd expansion?"

That was more responsibility than Geoff had been expecting, but if Jarvis was that buried, it might be better. "You'll need to detail what exactly overseeing his expansion means, and I'll need to meet with him before agreeing to anything."

"That's reasonable." Jarvis started walking again, this time with a slight bounce to his step. "This will be excellent. It'll free me up for when I talk to Lord Broughton."

"This is supposed to free you up for your estate and working with Lord Thurston."

"It does, tremendously." He hopped up on the edge of a low rock wall. "But I want to think towards the future."

"How about handling the present?"

"If I can sway Lord Broughton from Mr. Udayle's ear, he'd be an excellent ally. He has many of the older, smaller, established millworks in his corner."

"It seems you have more than enough business to be satisfied for a while." Geoff narrowed his eyes. "Unless this is less about business and more about Mr. Udayle."

"Upending Udayle does give me a great deal of pleasure." Jarvis hopped off the wall and began walking through the grassy lawn. Or used to be grassy. There were brown patches throughout it currently.

"This is too big to descend into some petty war between you and a childhood nemesis. I have half a mind to pull out now."

"No, please don't. At least not before you've considered everything thoroughly. I've already been warned by an investor, and I'm sure you'll check me."

"Maybe you ought to consider a board of sorts if you need people to check you."

Jarvis made a face. "I like calling the shots."

"But if you shoot yourself, what good is it?"

"Good point. I'll consider it." He stopped short at a flower bed and seemed to critically examine one of the patches of flowers. "This won't do," he muttered.

Geoff tried to figure out to what he was alluding, for the section appeared fine to him. It was one of the few he'd seen that didn't appear on its last leg.

"Now, I'm supposed to meet with the architect in a bit to discuss the north wing because it's in near collapse," Jarvis said. "Would you like to accompany me?"

"Certainly. But again, don't embark on too much, Jarvis. You'll burn out and possibly hurt others in the process."

Jarvis clapped him on the back. "I'll be fine. I'm turning that wing into my greenhouse and arboretum. Complete with an extensive library and plenty of places to store seeds, bulbs, and start seedlings. It'll be marvelous."

"Yes, it's good to take up activities that relax and focus you."

"And now that Clive has his own shipping man, I could probably get him to fetch me more unusual varieties. The possibilities are practically endless."

Geoff sighed as they walked towards the north wing of the house.

"Let's discuss a different topic of interest," Jarvis said. "Another London season passes, and one of this area's most eligible bachelors is still not snatched?" He grinned. "When will you award a winner? Who will be the fortunate lady upon whom you bestow this gift?"

"You speak astounding nonsense sometimes. Last week, I began courting Miss Faye."

Jarvis seemed surprised. "She's lovely in an exotic way."

Geoff narrowed his eyes. "She's lovely. Period."

"Yes, of course. Her looks are just—"

"Jarvis, there is no possible way you can continue that line of thought in a sensible manner, so I suggest you end it."

"Excellent suggestion. I take it Miss Faye has a substantial dowry."

Geoff stared at him.

"Not to say that's the only reason you'd court her," Jarvis rushed on. "She has many other fine qualities—"

"Please change the subject."

"Right. We might actually see a touch of sun this afternoon after all."

*****

Coordinating a visit with Lord Vaughnryd in Derbyshire was more difficult. It would be almost a week to travel there and back, and Lord Vaughnryd was recently married. He actually resided at Corwyn, but since their business was primarily connected with Vaughnryd, he wanted to meet Geoff there.

Geoff didn't get to the lake areas and peak district too often, so he was excited to travel to the region but anxious about being away from Faye. His absence and Clive's proximity this early in their courtship might end things for him before he began in earnest.

Jarvis's primary mission was to outfit Lord Vaughnryd's mills with the new looms so they could produce more specialized damask. How that was accomplished, he left up to Geoff as long as he was kept in the loop.

Vaughnryd reminded Geoff of Hartwell, but on a smaller scale, and it was kept in tip-top shape. The earl appeared to have his affairs in order, and Geoff could understand why Jarvis was excited to collaborate with him.

After entering through an impressive porch and entrance hall, Geoff was joined by Lord Vaughnryd in the drawing room. He was of average height with dark brown hair and hazel eyes and carried himself with the same confidence and poise the estate exuded.

"Welcome to Vaughnryd." The earl shook Geoff's hand, and the two men took seats.

"Thank you for allowing me to come. I know this is a hectic time for you."

"Your involvement may make it less so if Duke Hartwell wasn't exaggerating. What are you offering me? The Duke and Lord Thurston had agreed to take over operations of my mills so I could concentrate on the quarries and building materials."

"Duke Hartwell has asked me to oversee the expansion of your mill with the new looms."

"It would appear he promised too much."

"In his defense, the death of his father and subsequent inheritance was largely unforeseen. Otherwise, he wouldn't have put things in motion as he did."

Lord Vaughnryd smiled faintly. "You're telling me to lighten up on him?"

Geoff chuckled. "I agree with proceeding cautiously and empathize with your exasperation, but his current predicament is partially a result of circumstances beyond his control."

Lord Vaughnryd led Geoff to his office in a different wing and introduced him to his steward, who discussed things as they stood.

Geoff felt overwhelmed. He'd researched the industry before his departure, but to be square in the middle of an actual working operation was an entirely different matter.

"I'm not like Lord Thurston," Lord Vaughnryd remarked. "I have no interest in developing a domestic textile empire."

"Nor I, and hopefully that's not what the ultimate goal is."

"I may exaggerate," the earl conceded. "But Lord Thurston is into dominance and making a lot of money. I am not. My mills are strictly a means to employ those that live on or near the estate and provide the area with needed goods."

"I understand, and my brother had said as much."

"But you're probably not the best man to oversee operations."

"Correct, and I made that clear to Lord Spalding and Duke Hartwell. My role is only to direct the expansion, not the operations of the mill itself."

"My steward usually sees to the daily operations since it comes under the affairs of the estate at large. He communicates with the two managers at the mills, and I execute major decisions. The system has worked thus far but would probably deteriorate under a heavier workload. With an expansion, a foreman similar to the one Lord Thurston has at his largest mill would be ideal."

"Then perhaps I could include hiring one as part of the project."

"That would be tremendously helpful. What do you think so far? Are you ready to take me on?"

Geoff nodded. "I think the two of us will get on better than you and Duke Hartwell."

Lord Vaughnryd smirked. "Agreed. Why don't we take a ride to the mills, and you can see things firsthand."

*****

The mills were four miles southeast of the house proper and about two miles apart. On the way there, Geoff inquired after Lord Vaughnryd's new wife, Lady Corwyn, and his demeanor changed completely.

"She might be more helpful and encouraging," Lord Vaughnryd said. "She's more open-minded about this arrangement than I am."

"As I understand, her estate is nearby."

"Yes, we were neighbors. You'll be there this evening. While I wished to meet at Vaughnryd, we fully intended to have you stay with us at Corwyn."

"Thank you. I appreciate that." Geoff paused, not sure how much he wanted to open up. "I recently began a courtship with a lady who lives very close to me as well."

"Who is the lady in question?"

"Miss Faye Armstrong of Oakes Hollow."

"I'm not acquainted with Miss Armstrong personally, but I've heard Oakes Hollow is a wonderful park to tour. I believe she's connected to Mr. George Sabo, with whom I am acquainted."

Geoff was surprised. "Yes, he's her maternal grandfather. How do you know him?"

"I sell coal through his shop in Liverpool. My grandfather established the arrangement, and I've kept it."

"Small world." Geoff was glad he made the disclosure, as it made him more comfortable. "I've never met Mr. Sabo, but the Armstrongs speak highly of him."

"Yes, from what my grandfather told me, it's been arduous for Mr. Sabo to establish the thriving coal shop and good-sized home he owns. He's defied the odds in being seen as a well-respected man in his neighborhood and not just by the small African community there."

They arrived at the first mill, a single-story stone building. The steward introduced Geoff to the manager.

"This mill does predominantly linen, though we make a small amount of wool," the manager said as they stood just inside the doorway.

"Each mill employs about 50 people. The cotton and flax arrive already processed. We spin and weave it into thread, yarn, and fabric using a combination of jennies, power looms, and water frames," the steward explained. "We also have a couple of seamstresses to make finished products like pants and shirts."

"As ambivalent as I was about the enterprise, the fabric this new loom can produce is impressive,"

Lord Vaughnryd admitted. "I'd be excited to have such pieces readily available for my community. But they intimated the skill needed to run the looms is advanced."

"It can be learned, but the system used is quite different from anything we've ever seen. Lord Thurston's foreman, Mr. Edgar Locke, has mastered and taught it to others, but it's a different way of communicating to the machine that creates more ornate patterns."

"Sounds too much to me. I rather stick with my limestone blocks and building."

"The upshot is whoever is hired must be willing to learn something different and learn it well since Mr. Locke is not from these parts."

"Understood. You have a better handle on this than you let on."

"I understand the framework, but I don't know the details, and those are important."

Lord Vaughnryd nodded.

"I suggest we add rather than replace, and then your current operation can remain intact while we're sorting out the new," Geoff continued. "It appears you have a small, tight system in place, and I believe we should test how these looms will change things before going larger."

"Yes, I don't want a surplus of product I can't sell or sky-high costs."

"I assumed there were plans in place for the increase."

"I did too, but nothing definitive has been arranged along those lines, and you know where assumptions can lead."

Geoff nodded. "Do you work much with silk? Or will your damask and brocade be cotton?"

"I have no silk mills."

"If you're not opposed, we can head to the cotton mill. It might be best to build the addition there."

"I can easily put you in contact with architects and builders," Lord Vaughnryd offered as Geoff studied the land by the second mill. "Any materials you need are at your disposal."

"Excellent. The looms are extraordinarily pricey, though I believe they're working on the design to bring those costs down. Are you comfortable investing in two?"

"That'll be Lady Corwyn's department. I believe she has already made funding available. If the costs exceed her initial investment, we may need to re-evaluate. I don't want to run through her resources and mine."

"I'll be moderate, but I gather you'd want a decent environment for those who work for you."

"Absolutely, but keep it simple."

"Done."

*****

Geoff was impressed with the orphan turned countess, in her own right, Lady Corwyn. As he had heard, the countess was a stunning woman, a clear porcelainlike complexion, with vibrant blue eyes, and black hair. She had a restful air to her that Geoff appreciated as well.

"Lord Vaughnryd warned me you'd pepper me with questions this evening," Lady Corwyn said after they'd settled in the drawing room after dinner.

"I don't wish to mar your evening. We can discuss business tomorrow."

"It's fine to begin, and that'll give me time to reflect on anything weightier."

"We'd like you to invest in two looms," Geoff said bluntly.

"I see no immediate problem with that," Lady Corwyn replied. "Will it exceed the funding I've already made available?"

"It shouldn't, as you outlaid a good deal to start."

"Yes, my guardian's parting gift was much larger than I ever expected."

"But it'll be a sizeable chunk, and we've decided to build an addition instead of replacing older, existing looms."

"Ah, I see. Will you start immediately?"

"I think the sooner I begin, the better."

"By your departure, we'll make sure you have what you need to accomplish your tasks." Lady Corwyn glanced at Lord Vaughnryd, who nodded.

"Lady Corwyn, you seemed to have assumed your new role very capably."

She grinned. "I had a very excellent tutor."

CHAPTER 11

The Warning

Faye

FAYE'S FATHER FOUND HER on a bench in the gardens some distance from the house. "You have a letter from Mr. Fitzpatrick."

Faye took it from him, surprised, for she expected no such thing from Geoff. While he'd be away for some little time, it wasn't as though it'd be weeks and months. "Thank you. That was quite kind of you to personally deliver it to me out here."

"I thought you'd want to read it as soon as possible. Enjoy."

Faye stared after him as he walked off whistling. Lady Yardley wouldn't be the only one upset if she discovered the true nature of their courtship. Her father had been positively thrilled when they'd told him.

She watched the water cascade down the stone steps into the lake below and then opened the letter. *It's nice to receive a letter from him.* She grinned and began reading.

Faye chuckled at his disbelief in how much responsibility he'd just been handed. She frowned at Geoff's description of Duke Hartwell embarking on too much. His eagerness to be together again warmed her.

Faye sat back and held the letter close to her. *Maybe I'll see if I can read about mills, looms, and things since Geoff will be so involved with it. I don't want to sound like a silly goose when speaking with him.*

She walked up the stairs of the path. *I've never been concerned with whether I sound like a silly goose with Clive. A silly goose might be what he prefers.*

That didn't sit well with her.

Faye shook her head. *Clive is a splendid match for me. I just have to convince him. But meanwhile, I can enjoy my time with Geoff.*

*****

A few days later, Geoff walked into the drawing room, a smile lighting his face.

I could get used to his sunshine smiles. Faye grinned back, laying her book to the side. "It's good to see you. When did you return home?"

"Yesterday."

"And you're here to call upon me today? Don't you want a couple of days' rest?"

"I'll rest after I leave here." He paused. "I did want to see you."

"Is anything the matter?"

"No. I just wished to see you."

"How lovely. I decided to do some reading on mills since you're to be so involved with them."

"I'm pleased you've taken an interest in my project. I can bring some material that you're welcome to read the next time I come."

"Thank you. How's Clive? What is he up to?"

Faye thought she saw a ghost of a frown, but it was gone before it fully formed. "He's well enough, I suppose. He's actually at Spalding today."

A pity. Faye shook her head. *I'll need to stop feeling that way so sharply if this bizarre plan is to work.*

"Is anything the matter?" Geoff asked.

"No." *I need a distraction.* "Why don't we do a sculpture sit-in?"

After following her into the studio, he took a seat by one of the windows and stared outside.

Faye suddenly felt nervous and busied herself with putting on an apron. She rarely sculpted in the dresses she received callers, but she hadn't planned on this session. Besides, they were courting, and she'd rather not have her suitor see her in a work dress.

My suitor.

Faye glanced at Geoff as she tied her hair back with a series of strips of cloth. She had been excited from an artist's point of view to sculpt him, but at this moment, she saw him through female eyes. Faye had always acknowledged he was good-looking, but now she was struck with just how greatly. It was one of the few times she was spending time with Geoff without Clive, and she supposed Clive had always taken her attention.

"I see you have a sculpting uniform," he remarked.

"Things get messy. As much as Father loves to buy me dresses, I don't want to make it a weekly endeavor for him. I apologize for this overcoat is not in the best of shape."

"I think it's fine and suits you very well."

"Thank you."

"Your father must support your sculpting whole-heartedly. This is a wonderful space."

"Yes, he's very good to me."

"Was your mother artistic?"

"She was always singing. Her grandpapa was a violin prodigy."

"Fascinating. Do you know much about him?"

Faye loved talking about her family, and she didn't get to do it too often. "Mama told me he played his way free. The captain of the ship he played on brought him to his home as a servant, and eventually, he earned enough through his playing to buy his freedom. Family legend has it some great composer made a song just for him to play, but that's probably Williams' folklore."

Geoff pointed towards a statue. "And that bust of your grandfather is Mr. George Sabo?"

Faye nodded. "He was on a sugar plantation until the owner sent him to the family estate here, after Grandpapa learned figures. The plantation owner was storied to have had a child by one of the slaves, and he freed all of them when he died."

Geoff nodded, looking grave.

"So Grandfather Sabo went into business and is apparently very, very good at it."

"Yes, Lord Vaughnryd mentioned him, for he does some coal business with Mr. Sabo."

"And you? What family history does yours have?"

"Someone involved in the Norman conquest, I believe. A cartographer. A couple of royal advisers." He gave her a rueful smile. "I should know more than I do."

"Never too late to learn." She clapped her hands. "Let's see what we can do with you today." Her female brain went off, and her artist's brain clicked on as she surveyed him critically. Faye slowly circled him, her mind calculating what he'd be like in sculpture form. Ways she could bring him to life.

"You're incredibly unnerving right now."

Faye blinked. "What am I doing?"

"Your scrutiny. Are you peeling me apart layer by layer?"

Faye grinned. "I did have some studies in anatomy that were most helpful. I have the book if you'd like to see it—"

"No, no. I'm fine."

Faye forced back a giggle. "I didn't mean to make you uncomfortable. I'm just trying to plot my composition."

"Dissecting your subject?"

"I'll humanize you next session."

Geoff chuckled.

They had a brief discussion on what materials she could use for the sculpture.

"I'll leave that decision to you." Geoff grinned. "If you decide to use limestone, I have sources now that I'm working closely with Lord Vaughnryd."

Faye's girl brain suddenly clicked on again. *That grin will be the death of me. Why have I never noticed how incredibly handsome Geoff is?* "If you can stay, I'd like to do some sketches."

"Of course. I'm entirely at your disposal."

Faye's stomach dropped. *Something about the way he said that...*

She rushed around getting her drawing materials.

*****

Aunt Bonnie sat next to Faye on the couch after supper. "I saw that Mr. Geoffrey stayed with you all afternoon today. He must have missed you a great deal while he was away."

"No, not at all; I can assure you, Aunt Bonnie."

"Now you're being overly modest."

"I'm quite in earnest. I'm sure he didn't miss me any more than usual, if at all."

Aunt Bonnie studied her. "Why would you say that?"

Faye continued scribbling on her pad. She was filling in details and shading on Geoff's sketch. His serious face stared back at her. *I rather wish you had missed me to that degree.* She lightly traced the outline of his face. *Will you allow me to see your real likeness?*

"Faye, what is going on?" Aunt Bonnie asked.

She laid down her pencil. "If I tell you something, promise not to tell anyone."

Aunt Bonnie narrowed her eyes. "I'm not a young girl anymore. It depends on what this disclosure is."

Faye swallowed. "Our courtship isn't real."

"Not real? Are you two not courting?"

"We are, but it's not like we actually like one another."

Aunt Bonnie appeared perplexed. "There are those that court that aren't exactly taken with one another, but I'd find that circumstance hard to believe in your case. I'm fairly certain Mr. Geoffrey cares for you a great deal, and I can't imagine you're indifferent towards him."

"I'm not. I care for him as well, just not in that way." Faye twiddled her hands. "The one I really like is Clive, and Geoff offered to court me to make him jealous."

Aunt Bonnie seemed deep in thought.

"It sounded like a crazy idea to me too when Geoff had first proposed the plan."

"So this was initially his idea?"

Faye nodded. "So you see, he's not courting me to really court me."

"And what did Mr. Geoffrey tell you he has to gain by this so-called charade? Besides the obvious?"

"The obvious?"

"Actually winning your true affection," Aunt Bonnie answered like she was daft.

"Oh, that. No, he enjoys the idea of rankling Clive for some reason."

Aunt Bonnie frowned. "Disaster is written all over it, Faye. This kind of deceitfulness can only lead to—"

"Deceitful!" Faye cried out. "We are actually courting, and I daresay Geoff and I have greater affection for one another than many couples."

"Exactly," her aunt replied firmly. "Which is why I feel this ruse will lead to no good in the end, and you may jeopardize something very good."

"I'm sure it won't come to that. I'll be careful."

Aunt Bonnie pressed her lips together. "You're of age and allowed to make your own decisions in these matters." She rose. "I must see to the jam preparation."

"Of course."

Her aunt was seldom disappointed in her, and Faye's heart was heavy as she watched her walk away. *But Aunt Bonnie's pronouncement sounded so dire. Things might not turn out quite the way I'd envisioned, but nothing will seriously go wrong, will it?*

CHAPTER 12

Caught

Faye

"**L**ADY HELENA IS HERE to see you, Miss Faye," the butler announced the next day.

Faye laid her sewing down. Ordinarily, she'd welcome a distraction from that task but was surprised and mildly suspicious about this visit. "I'll go to her directly."

The Gillinghams and Armstrongs called on one another occasionally, but Lady Helena had never sought Faye's company on her own. Since Faye had seen her at the dinner and the dance a few weeks prior, she was curious as to why Lady Helena bothered to call on her now.

"You seemed keen to accompany us on our trip, so I thought I'd stop and conduct an initial interview," Lady Helena explained as Faye took a seat in the drawing room.

"I didn't realize you'd do such a thing, though I suppose that makes sense."

"Mama and I want to make sure we have the best, and I do enjoy surprise and candid questionings. Find out what people are really about."

"Ask away. I'm at your ready command."

"If you could first fetch me a glass of water; I'm so thirsty for some reason."

That's not exactly what I meant by at your command. Deciding to ignore Lady Helena's tone, Faye poured her a glass of water from the sideboard and then sat back down again.

Lady Helena took a sip and then gave an exaggerated shiver. "There must be a draft or something in here. Do you have a shawl or something? My constitution is quite delicate."

Faye fought an eye roll and busied herself with retrieving a light blanket from the shelves in the anteroom. "Will this do?"

"I suppose. I guess it's my fault for not bringing one of my nice wraps."

Faye tried not to make a face as she handed her the blanket and sat again.

It took five more minutes for Lady Helena to finish her water and situate herself. Finally, she began a litany of questions, half of which Faye didn't understand what the information had to do with the trip.

There was a knock, and then the butler entered. "Lord Spalding and Mr. Fitzpatrick are here. Shall I show them in or ask them to wait, if they're able, until you are available?"

Their timing couldn't have been better, but I shouldn't appear overeager to be rid of Lady Helena. "Perhaps if they could wait in the—"

"Don't make them wait on my account," Lady Helena cut in coolly. "I'd love to visit with Lord Spalding and Mr. Fitzpatrick. That is, if you could be convinced to share them."

The butler gave an almost imperceptible raise of his eyebrow.

Faye bit the side of her cheek to keep from saying something very naughty in return and, instead, told the butler the brothers could join them.

Lady Helena sat up straighter and removed the blanket from around her shoulders. "If you're so busy with the men, perhaps I should investigate other companions."

Faye set her jaw. "You're aware that I'm courting Mr. Fitzpatrick, so a call from him in the company of his brother shouldn't seem extraordinary. But if you'd rather have a companion that is not engaged in that way, of course, you must choose what is in your best interests."

"I see the way you look at Lord Spalding."

Faye froze.

"Which is curious given you're in a courtship with his younger brother." Lady Helena shot her a wicked smile. "What happened, Faye dear? Not quite good enough for the heir?"

Faye gritted her teeth.

The smirk vanished from Lady Helena's face. "If you ruin my chances with Lord Spalding, you can kiss the trip goodbye. It's almost worth taking you just to make sure you behave while we're gone. We'll see what kind of performance you're about to put on."

Lady Helena is about to see the theatrical of a lifetime. Faye hopped up when the brothers entered the room and grabbed Geoff's hands. She leaned over as though to kiss him and then stopped short, giggling. "I almost forgot myself." She squeezed his hands. "This will have to do. I'm so delighted you've come."

Geoff appeared amused. "I'm glad to be here."

"Two days in a row," Faye gushed. "You'll have people believing you can't live without me."

"I can't."

Faye gave him a playful swat on the arm even as her stomach dropped. *He's good. That sounded real.*

"Come now, Mr. Fitzpatrick," said Lady Helena. "It's early in your courtship for those kinds of pronouncements."

"Perhaps. But that doesn't make them less true."

He is outstanding.

Clive gave them a curious look and then asked Lady Helena about her mother.

Geoff guided Faye towards the window, which seemed to distract Clive from his conversation. "You're fortunate Lady Helena doesn't know you well, or she would have seen right through that," he said quietly with a faint smile.

Faye let out a soft groan. "She suspects something is amiss, though Clive seems to have bought into it. He's glanced over here twice."

"He bought me."

"You're very convincing," Faye agreed. "I had no idea you possessed such superior acting skills."

Geoff was quiet for a moment. "Why is it so difficult to imagine that I could genuinely care for you?"

"I know you care for me. But in that way? It's hard to imagine you caring for anyone in that manner."

His face grew blank. "So you think me incapable of loving another?"

"No, of course not. That was incredibly rude of me. You don't express a great deal of affection, and it's just hard to get to know you. You keep to yourself."

"That's true. So you don't think you know me?"

"I do," She paused, trying to figure out how to explain her thoughts. "It's like there's Mr. Fitzpatrick and then there's Geoff. I feel I don't know Geoff as well as I'd like, and it's completely different from how I wish to know my husband."

"I'll have to reflect upon that." He paused. "I imagine you're closer to Clive than his Lord Spalding. But you believe you could know Clive in the manner you described?"

Faye opened her mouth and then shut it again. *Hit acknowledged.* "I'm embarrassed to say I never thought that far with regards to him."

"Never thought that far regarding me in what, Faye?" Clive asked behind her.

Faye jumped, having been so involved in her conversation with Geoff that she hadn't noticed Clive walk towards them.

"You must share, Miss Faye." Lady Helena stood next to Clive.

"Surely you don't expect Miss Faye to share words meant only for her suitor," said Geoff.

"And my name came up?" Clive asked. "You must do better than that, Geoff."

Clive's tone bothered Faye, and she stepped closer to Geoff. "It would seem he did fine since he had my undivided attention, and I quite forgot you were even in the room."

Geoff smugly crossed his arms.

Clive gave them another curious look.

"Our call today has a purpose," Geoff said to Faye. "Mother invited a harpist to play for us tomorrow afternoon and asked if you were available to join. We thought you might enjoy the string music given your connections."

Faye beamed. "I absolutely accept. What a lovely invitation."

"I adore the harp as well," chimed in Lady Helena. "Such ethereal music."

"I'm sure you'd be most welcome too," Clive said. "Your mother as well."

"Excellent. We'll be there," she replied as the clock bells sounded. "The time has quite escaped me. Would you gentlemen be so kind as to escort me home? I had walked here for a little exercise."

"Of course, we're at your service," Clive responded.

The two started for the door, and he looked back towards Geoff. "Coming?"

"I'll be along in a second, brother."

"Let the lovebirds say goodbye," Lady Helena said in a mocking voice.

Faye growled after she walked out of the room.

"I apologize for not waiting until she was at least out of earshot to deliver Mother's invitation," Geoff said. "I was excited to share it and had no notion Lady Helena would be interested in that sort of thing."

"She probably didn't either until you issued the invitation."

Geoff laughed.

"That was quite mean of me," Faye said. "There's no reason to believe she wouldn't like that kind of music any more than we do."

"There was more to mother's invitation. If you could favor us with spending the weekend, as our musical guest will stay the night with her parents. The harpist is the daughter of a viscount and our age. Mother hopes you two will enjoy one another's company."

"That sounds delightful and very thoughtful of your mother." She sobered. "I'm so afraid of disappointing her. Aunt Bonnie is already upset with me."

"Aunt Bonnie knows of our situation?"

"Listen to you call her Aunt Bonnie."

Geoff turned a touch pink. "I'm usually more careful, but I do think of her that way. She fusses over me so."

"I don't mind at all; I think it's rather adorable. You can call her Aunt Bonnie. It's just me."

Geoff gazed at her for a moment. "You say that like it's a little thing."

Faye felt flushed. "You don't have to pretend when it's just me either. We've never been like that."

"No. Never." He paused. "And I'm not pretending now."

The butler walked in, looking apologetic. "I'm sorry, Miss Faye and Mr. Fitzpatrick, but Lord Spalding seems quite eager to depart."

Faye and Geoff looked at one another and burst out laughing.

"Clive and I will be here at noon to escort you back to our home for the festivities if that's agreeable to you," Geoff said.

Faye bobbed her head. "Absolutely. Thank your mother again. I can't wait."

Geoff took her hand. "Have a good afternoon."

CHAPTER 13

A Musical Evening

Geoff

GEOFF REFLECTED UPON his conversation with Faye for the thousandth time as he put the finishing touches on his outfit. It was troublesome that she saw him as a gentleman who couldn't be enamored with a lady.

No wonder she's never looked at me. Not that he'd completely change himself for her, but Faye needed to be close to her partner, and he wasn't one for letting people be close to him. He was silly for not putting that together. He shouldn't have made Faye feel bad for not thinking the same point through concerning Clive.

Let her in, Geoff. Faye won't hurt you.

Clive and he set out shortly thereafter.

"You two are really taking things far," Clive said.

"It's interesting you'd assume I'm not serious about our courtship just because you've never considered her as a suitor. I told you before you're the one hurting her because you won't give her the time of day."

"I talk to Faye all the time."

"Why wouldn't you consider her?"

Clive shrugged. "I just haven't. She's not my type."

"You have a type?"

"I don't chase every girl I see."

"No, but you're definitely a man of the people."

"You should try it. It might stop you from being so curmudgeonly."

"I'm quiet. That doesn't make me a curmudgeon."

"That was true when we were younger, but it's not anymore. What's happened to you?"

I don't know. I only know I'm tired of Clive.

"Do you really think Faye looks at me like that?" Clive questioned.

Geoff gave him a look.

"Then why is she courting you?" Clive asked as the carriage stopped in front of Oakes Hollow.

"You noticed, didn't you? Maybe I'm a curmudgeon because you want what little I have." Geoff got out of the carriage.

Clive rushed after him. "What do you mean?"

Geoff kept walking towards the door.

Clive grabbed his arm. "What are you talking about? I don't do that."

Geoff gave him a measured look. "We'll see."

The door flew open, and Faye beamed at them. "Hello!"

Geoff smiled, his dark mood melting away as he offered his arm.

✳✳✳✳✳

Faye

The Fitzpatricks possessed an excellent ear for music and hosted many musical guests. Yardley had a fine music room, and it was a treat to be invited to concerts performed there.

Lady Yardley gave Faye another warm greeting and took her by the arm. "Let me borrow her for just a bit," she said to Geoff, "and then she's yours."

"Yes, mine." The briefest flicker of sadness crossed his face. "Certainly, Mama. I'll wait in the drawing room."

"Enjoy yourself this weekend," Lady Yardley said to Faye as they walked away. "I'm looking forward to hearing our guest. Her voice is supposed to be exquisite."

"I can't wait, and thank you for thinking of me in this kind manner."

"It's nothing. I was happy to do it, and this will give us the chance to become better acquainted in a different way. Geoff smiles more frequently after he began courting you."

"I didn't realize he smiled infrequently. He was always in decent humor when I've seen him."

"Now you know why."

If only that were true.

"He has much to offer but keeps himself tucked away," she continued. "His quietness is dear to me, but I want him to draw close to at least a few people, and I'm afraid he won't. I believe you can give him the courage and incentive to open up to others."

"Thank you," Faye replied. "You give me great credit."

I want to be the girl who'd do that for Geoff. Faye almost tripped. *That connection should be reserved for a girl who truly cares for him, and he for her, not me.*

They entered a grand guest room, and Lady Yardley took a seat by the bed. "I was delighted when Geoff told me of your great grandpapa. Is he still living?"

"No, he died when I was very young."

"A pity. I would've invited him to play. Did he pass his talents down?"

"Mama had a lovely voice, but I didn't inherit their musical abilities. I could only listen happily."

"But you're gifted artistically in other ways. Do you have opportunities to develop those talents further? I know you were schooled, but studies abroad would be ideal, though I suppose not the best choice at this time."

"I'd love to study in Italy or perhaps take a European tour. I'm hoping Lady Girnwood and her daughter will select me for their trip to Scotland."

Lady Yardley was quiet for a moment. "How do you get on with them?"

To speak poorly of a woman of nobility to another noblewoman was bad form, but Faye wanted to be open. "I believe many feel they're not the easiest pair to be closely acquainted, but we get on well enough."

"That's very diplomatic of you." Lady Yardley studied Faye. "Many underestimate your worth. Don't buy into that."

She had no notion that she did. "I'll remember that. Thank you."

"The Livingstons will arrive shortly, so we'll have time to get acquainted before the other guests arrive." She paused. "Lady Girnwood and Lady Helena will come later, closer to dinner and a performance afterward. When I was told of their attendance, I thought it best to condense things."

Faye hid a smile.

"I'm hoping to persuade Miss Livingston to play for us again tomorrow. Now, I'll take you back to Geoff before he comes searching for us."

*****

Geoff beamed when Faye walked in. "Would you take a turn with me?"

"Absolutely." She glanced at Clive sitting in the corner. "Would you like to come too?"

He rose. "Indeed, I would."

Geoff scowled at him for a second before his face cleared.

"What do you have planned for this autumn, Faye?" Geoff asked once they were outdoors.

"It's not London, but I'm always one for the usual round of parties and get-togethers."

Geoff winced.

"Go on, and show your undying devotion to your suitor, Geoff." Clive snickered. "Faye and Daisy's circuit might kill you."

Faye glared at him and then turned her attention back towards Geoff, slipping her arm through his. "But we don't have to do that always. Spending time with you privately would be fine too. I want to do what you enjoy as well."

Faye was surprised at how heartfelt that sentiment was. Just a month ago, she was determined to spend as much time as possible in Clive's company.

"I'm sure we could reach a compromise," Geoff said.

"Anytime it gets too much for Geoff, I'd be happy to fill in," Clive offered.

Geoff's jaw clenched.

"Thank you," Faye responded evenly. *Why am I so cool towards Clive? He's the one I want to spend time with, right?*

"Are you ready for Lady Helena, brother?" Geoff smirked.

Clive glared at him as Faye chuckled. *Wait, that's not funny. Lady Helena has a real chance with him. Or maybe not based on his facial expression. But this is good practice for when she comes. I'm truly behaving like I want to be with Geoff, though this doesn't feel like I'm acting.* Faye shook her head as though to clear it. "Tell me about your trip to Derbyshire. I've never been."

"We'll have to visit sometime. The lake and peak districts are sublime." Geoff grinned at her. "Perfect for an artistic bent of mind such as yourself."

Faye's stomach flipped. *That grin could make me forget almost anything.* "That sounds wonderful."

"It's also forlorn out there," Clive said, intruding on the moment. "Perfect for the hermit bent of mind like Geoff."

"Clive," Faye said sternly.

"What?" he asked in mock innocence.

"That's all right, Faye. We can leave him with Lady Helena. They can go calling together."

Clive scowled.

"What ails you, brother?" Geoff asked. "Lady Helena not your type?"

The two brothers shared a dark look Faye had never seen on either of them before.

She cleared her throat. "Perhaps we should head inside so we're available when the others arrive." She dropped Geoff's arm and headed towards the house.

*****

Miss Phoebe Livingston walked beside Faye as the group made their way to the dining room. Their musical guest was talented and pretty, with a sunny but polished air that Faye admired.

"You played and sang beautifully," Faye said to her.

"Thank you," Miss Livingston replied. "I hear you sculpt. What a marvelous gift."

Lady Helena rushed up along Miss Livingston's other side. "But I've always preferred singing. It's cleaner and more feminine."

Faye bit the side of her cheek to prevent a retort.

Miss Livingston glanced between them. "We all possess our unique gifts, special in their own way."

"Marvelously worded," said Lady Helena. "Lord Spalding, what gift do you prefer?"

A slow smile spread across his face. "The gift of true friendship is priceless, and Miss Faye has bestowed that present most generously."

Lady Helena looked at her sharply.

That was a thoughtful response but an unusual one from Clive. She slipped her arm through Geoff's.

He tugged her closer. "I think you're trying too hard, Lord Spalding. Whom are you attempting to impress?"

"I certainly am," said Lady Girnwood. "There are some who'd say they've met no one as friendly as my dear Helena."

Geoff made a noise that resembled laughter, and Faye nudged him. The noise immediately morphed into coughing.

"Oh my, do you require water, Mr. Fitzpatrick?" asked Lady Girnwood.

"Yes, that was a bit hard to swallow."

Faye nudged him again.

"My mint," he blurted out. "It went down the wrong way."

Lady Girnwood nodded but gave him a curious look.

"Behave," Faye whispered to him when Lady Girnwood faced forward again.

"I'm trying," he murmured. "But she nearly killed me."

"You're so dramatic."

"I'm perfectly serious." His eyes glittered with mischief. "That mint could have choked me."

Faye giggled.

"Whispering sweet nothings into Mr. Fitzpatrick's ear, Miss Faye?" Lady Helena asked. "I do hate when courting couples are affectionate in public."

"I quite agree," said her mother as they entered the dining room. "Displays a complete lack of decorum."

"I believe there was nothing indecorous about my son's behavior," Lady Yardley said coolly.

"Of course not," Lady Girnwood gushed. "It's just sometimes those with whom we're in close company may expose us to bad habits."

"Such as backbiting and petty commenting?" Geoff asked.

Faye's eyes grew wide, but since she was three seats down from him, she couldn't give a look or nudge again.

"That's poor behavior indeed." Clive gave Geoff a level look. "But I'm sure no one here would act in a false manner."

"Or covet what another has," Geoff fired back.

Faye rubbed her forehead.

Miss Livingston glanced at Faye, appearing mildly amused.

Lord Yardley looked between his sons as he and then the rest of the company sat down. "I suggest we eat before the food grows cold."

*****

Thankfully, Lady Girnwood and Lady Helena departed for the night soon after dinner. Clive was attentive towards Faye when they gathered in the drawing room. But instead of soaking up his attention,

Faye kept looking for Geoff, who seemed to be enjoying his discussion with Miss Livingston.

Faye felt a flare of annoyance and then guilt. *That's not fair. Geoff was doing this for me, so I could do exactly what's occurring now. It's like I'm never satisfied regarding these two anymore.*

"I can let you be with Geoff if I'm boring you," Clive said, breaking her thoughts.

"No, of course not. I'm perfectly happy to speak with you."

"He had it in his head that you might fancy me."

Faye froze. *Geoff disclosed that? What is wrong with him?*

"You should have told me if that were true, though I can't imagine it would be."

"And what would've happened if I had?"

Clive shrugged.

"Exactly," Faye said with an edge.

"So he was right?"

She stood. "He was. I might fancy you, or I might not, but I'm definitely with him at present."

Faye strode over to Geoff, who was now alone.

"What on earth did you say to Clive?" Geoff chuckled. "It's been a long time since I've seen that many emotions fly across his face."

"Good. Serves him right." She punched Geoff's arm. "What do you mean by telling him I liked him?"

"He moved rapidly."

"What?"

"I knew he'd do something, but that was quicker than expected. For the record, I wasn't explicit; I only hinted."

"So you believed you were assisting me?"

"He's paying you a great deal of attention." Geoff paused. "Is he not your goal?"

"I suppose," she responded weakly.

Geoff studied her a moment. "If you wish to change objectives, you certainly could."

"Would you prefer that?"

"Yes."

Faye's stomach dropped. "I might need more time to be so definitive. That's a new thought and change of plans." *But not one I'm upset about.*

Geoff smiled. "Yes, I know how hard it is for you to think of me as an ardent suitor."

Faye felt flushed. *It seems he does that to me constantly now.* "Geoff..."

"I'm teasing," he said gently. "It's perfectly reasonable for you to think that way, and I promise I'll work harder at letting you get to know me better."

CHAPTER 14

Letting Her In

Faye

AFTER THE LIVINGSTONS LEFT Yardley on Monday morning, Geoff escorted Faye home and stayed for another sculpture session.

Since he could afford it, Faye had decided a milky-white translucent marble would suit Geoff's bust, and the finished work would be a true to size piece from the shoulders up. She was currently working on the clay model over an armature.

After a while, Faye stepped back and threw her hands up in the air in disgust.

"What's wrong?" Geoff walked to the work in progress. "I think it's coming along nicely."

"It's not right. It's not you."

The two stared at the sculpture.

"Maybe you need a closer examination," Geoff suggested.

Faye wrinkled her brow. "Closer? You're sitting near enough to me now."

"Might it help to feel my face and become more familiar with the planes, lines, ridges, and contours?"

Faye swallowed. She had done so for the bust she made of her sculpture tutor while she attended school in London. The exercise enabled her to "see" how the clay should feel in her hands and be molded, resulting in a better piece. But her sculpture instructor was certainly not her suitor, Geoffrey Fitzpatrick.

Geoff commissioned a bust, and it's for me to produce the best product I can. "Yes, I've done so for works in the past. If you don't mind sitting down again, I think that would be easier."

Geoff took his seat, and Faye tentatively reached out and poked his cheek.

He grinned. "Are you all right?"

She nodded vigorously, her heart pounding.

He pulled her hand to the side of his face and held it there. "See. Not so bad."

She slowly lifted her other hand so she was holding his head in her hands, feeling him drop his defenses.

A wave of affection washed over her. *He trusts me enough to let me in.*

He closed his eyes, and she moved her hands, feeling free to explore the plains of his face. *Let's get to know Geoff.*

She rubbed a small scar she'd never noticed before, just below his ear. "What happened here? Tavern brawl?"

He chuckled. "I slipped jumping rocks in a creek when I was younger."

"You appear clean-shaven, but your face feels rough."

"Mine grows in quick. If I need to be squeaky clean, I have to do it twice a day. It's good my hair is light."

Faye had no idea about such things. She didn't believe her father shaved as much, but then she never really cared before. But she wanted to know everything about Geoff.

Everything.

She held back. This was a sculpture session, and it was quickly transforming into something else.

"Did that help?" he asked quietly, opening his eyes.

"Yes." But she didn't want to move her hands yet.

He grinned. "Good. I'm glad."

"Thank you. I know how hard this is for you."

"I'll try my hardest for you."

New Ideas

Geoff

LORD THURSTON SPENT a couple of days at Hartwell to break up his journey to London from his home in Somersetshire. He and Jarvis continued the trip together by visiting Clive at Spalding, where Geoff met up with them.

His first impression of Lord Thurston was the nobleman was everything he wasn't — dynamic presence and power. He was a marquess like Geoff's father with wavy dark auburn hair and bright sapphire blue eyes.

"So you're the one cleaning up after Jarvis?" Lord Thurston asked.

"We should have invited your clean-up man," Jarvis retorted. "I'm sure Mr. Locke would have much to say on the subject. Clean up might be too kind a term."

Lord Thurston whistled. "It seems I've hit upon a sore topic."

"I apologize," Jarvis said. "It's been much discussed lately."

"I heard you paid Lord Vaughnryd a visit recently," Lord Thurston said to Geoff. "How was it?"

"It went well," he replied. "I received authorization to buy the looms, and I'm corresponding with a surveyor and architect now."

"Good. It sounds like he's more willing to work with you than Jarvis." Lord Thurston gave Jarvis a wicked grin.

Geoff held in a laugh. It wasn't often he saw his friend get teased like this.

"Did he have candidates for the loom workers?" Lord Thurston asked.

"He did not say," Geoff answered. "I can inquire about that when I ask him about the best way to procure some marble."

"Marble? That seems rich for a mill," remarked Jarvis.

"The marble is for me, for my bust." Geoff hadn't wanted to divulge he was getting one done in front of Lord Thurston, but he'd inadvertently opened the door for the revelation.

"You're to get a bust done?" Jarvis asked, surprised. "Is that your father's doing?"

Geoff shook his head. "My commission."

"Who's to do it?"

"Miss Faye."

"Miss Faye sculpts?" Jarvis exclaimed.

"Indeed," Geoff replied. "She's quite accomplished."

"I'd say so. I knew she was artistically inclined but didn't know in what manner. Remarkable." Jarvis's face took on a faraway look.

His thinking look.

"Whatever it is you're plotting, stop," Clive commanded.

Jarvis assumed a visage of innocence. "Who says I'm plotting anything?"

"We know that look," Geoff said.

Lord Thurston chuckled.

"Do you think she'd be willing to show me her work?" Jarvis asked.

"I don't see why not," Geoff responded. "I can make arrangements if she is."

"Please. See if she'd be willing to show us her sculptures and give a tour of the much talked about grounds of Oakes Hollow."

*****

Faye

Faye was in the drawing room, repeatedly picking up objects while pacing and then sitting again.

"Would you calm down?" Daisy exclaimed.

"A duke requested to see my work," Faye repeated for what felt the hundredth time, hardly containing her excitement. "If Geoff's commission goes well, and the duke speaks favorably of my work, or dare I even dream commission a piece for himself, I could become the favored sculptress for nobility. A unique status that belonged to me due to my own endeavors."

Daisy smiled. "That would be special indeed."

The men arrived, and introductions were made.

Geoff smiled at Faye as they headed to the gardens. "You're practically glowing today."

"I'm so excited at this opportunity. Thank you, Geoff."

"I had little to do with it. I only made an off-hand-ed remark, and it grew from there."

"I'm sure you did more, and I'm very grateful for it."

"You should know by now how much I enjoy doing things for you."

Faye squeezed his arm, beaming.

Faye loved giving tours though she didn't have the opportunity to do it often, as they assigned this task to one of the servants. She was proud of Oakes Hollow and happy this was a part of her. After the gardens tour, Faye showed them her studio. As the afternoon drew to a close, Jarvis requested another meeting and for Faye to be present.

*****

Geoff

Geoff, Daisy, and Faye made the trip to Spalding the next day.

"Why can't you just stick with one idea?" Clive asked, perplexed.

On this rare occasion, Geoff was in complete agreement with his brother.

"Right now, we're just selling cloth," Jarvis replied. "If we show people what to do with the cloth, it might drive more sales."

"They already know what to do with the cloth," Geoff said.

"Where is your imagination?" Jarvis exclaimed. "You have none, and neither do most of the people, which is why we have to show them."

"I'd be careful underestimating your customer base," Lord Thurston warned.

"I'm not underestimating them. I'm just making calculated suggestions I'm sure they never thought of."

Lord Thurston rolled his eyes.

"How about doing something with that unused field you're renting from Lord Darton?" Clive suggested. "I don't even know why you did that."

"So I can have a small source of flax independent of others," Jarvis replied.

"And where's the flax?" Clive questioned.

"I'm working on that."

"You really just wish to have sculptures draped in fabric?" Geoff asked.

"Yes."

"That's a costly proposition," ventured Faye.

"I assumed since Geoff was having a bust done of himself, and you're doing a marvelous one for your grandfather, it wasn't horribly expensive," Jarvis said.

"You're speaking of my suitor and a close relation." Faye carefully explained the costs incurred by such a commission.

"Highway robbery!" Jarvis exclaimed.

Faye chuckled. "It takes quite a bit of time and skill, and the finished product is only a fraction of the size of the starting piece of material."

"I might have to rethink this," Jarvis said.

"Where were you planning on putting these fabric-wearing sculptures?" asked Clive.

"In our shop," answered Jarvis.

"We don't have a shop," said Clive.

"We will. You need to sell your merchandise anyway."

"I have contacts."

Jarvis gave him a look.

"Well, yes, I thought that would go smoother than it has," conceded Clive. "Who's to run this shop?"

"Fitz."

"No," Geoff retorted.

"But you've done stupendously with Vaughnryd's mill so far," Jarvis said.

"We've just started," Geoff replied. "I don't run shops."

"Just a tiny one. We can have a splendid setup in London. I'll speak with Lord Darton about it." He hopped up from his seat. "It could be a beau monde..." he paused. "We'll call it a boutique to make it sound cosmopolitan—"

Lord Thurston snorted. "It's fabric, Jarvis."

He waved him off. "It's all in how you wrap it. In our boutique, the rich choose their fabric, it's transformed by the seamstresses on site, and then they can have busts made of themselves modeling the results."

Geoff had to admit that sounded almost narcissistic enough to work.

"Who is to pay for all these statues?" Lord Thurston asked. "Because it won't be me."

"The rich can," Jarvis responded. "I'll make it the new thing. See a likeness of yourself modeling the latest fashion with the highest grade fabric in our exclusive boutique." He looked towards Faye. "I can get you a steady line of work."

Geoff frowned. "What makes you believe she requires a steady line of work? I'd find it hard to believe you'd make that sort of statement to another lady of her station."

"Some ladies liked to be occupied."

"There's a sizable difference between occupation and what you're suggesting," Geoff said.

"Geoff, I don't think he meant anything by it," Clive remarked.

"And therein lies the problem," he retorted.

"I did not intend to insult, Miss Faye," Jarvis said to her.

"Thank you, but Mr. Fitzpatrick's point is well made," she replied carefully. "I don't seek a life of leisure and do like to be occupied, but I sculpt primarily for my enjoyment. While I was excited at the possibility of sculpting for you, I'm not looking for steady work and choose my projects and commissions carefully."

"Of course, Miss Faye. And if you agreed to this arrangement, you would have full veto control over the projects. As a matter of fact, if it's popular, we'd have to be selective anyway." He grinned. "Exclusivity would make the idea even better."

"Why don't we table that scheme for now," suggested Lord Thurston. "I'm not completely sold on how advantageous it will be, and there would be much to work out if it comes to fruition."

"All right then, let's talk about departure and arrival to London in a few days," said Jarvis. "I think we should travel together. The four of us would make a fine show. Our carriages could roll in deep."

Daisy giggled.

Clive threw an arm around the back of his chair. "I like the sound of that."

"Do what you want," Lord Thurston said. "I don't care."

"Fitz?" Jarvis asked.

The men looked expectantly at him.

Geoff gave them a withering look. "What are you to do in London, and why do you need me?"

"Business, of which you are a part."

Geoff exhaled.

"Making a splash isn't up Geoff's alley," Clive commented.

"We need him," Jarvis said. "There's something to his person that sells the look and arrests people's attention."

"Me?" Geoff asked incredulously.

"You might try to disappear," Jarvis replied. "But people take note of you, and they're impressed. The rest of us have to act like idiots to get the attention back."

"Speak for yourself," Clive said.

"No, my friend, you are definitely idiot number one," retorted Jarvis. He looked at Geoff again. "You can bring the ladies. Might make the entourage look better."

"I'll spare them the spectacle," Geoff grumbled. "It's fine. I'll survive."

CHAPTER 16

The Fruit Festival

Faye

FAYE GAVE A CONTENTED SIGH as she viewed the gardens the following Monday. Their family held a fruit festival every year, which was Aunt Bonnie's special event, as she took a particular interest in the fruit orchards and even had a hand in selling the jams. Aunt Bonnie was a flutter because the Fitzpatrick brothers were bringing Duke Hartwell and Lord Thurston since they were still visiting Spalding. The group would leave for London the following day.

The festivities were held where many of the decorative fruit trees were planted, and featured jams, pies, sweetbreads, and meats. Faye was ready to indulge herself, and she was excited to share the selection of treats she'd prepared just for her and Geoff.

Daisy gave her a playful shove. "Stop daydreaming about your beau."

"How did you know I was thinking about him?

"You get this happy, faraway expression," Daisy explained. "I don't think you realize how often you're in that stupor. It's sweet, but we have things to do right now."

I care for Geoff more deeply than I ever realized.

Daisy shoved a fork full of cherry pie in her mouth.

"It's ten in the morning." Faye chuckled. "Where did you get that?"

"You think we can convince Aunt Bonnie to hold these back? I don't want to share."

The housekeeper handed Faye a note and a nosegay. "This just came for you from Yardley."

Faye squealed as she took her gifts.

"He was just here yesterday," Daisy commented.

"I know. This nosegay is lovely." Faye ripped open the note. Geoff invited her and Daisy to dine with him when he returned from London.

"Of course, I'll go with you," Daisy replied when Faye asked. "Knowing Geoff, he'll pamper you and then me by default."

Faye grinned as she started putting the flowers in her hair. *He does cater to me excellently.*

*****

The festivities were well underway, and Faye was playing a game of ring-toss with Geoff and another young boy when Lady Helena requested a few moments private conference with her. The gazebo was at the far end of the garden from the fruit trees, so Faye took her there, thinking that would be a comfortable location for a discussion.

"It was a difficult decision because there were many young ladies who were interested, and some of them very noteworthy," Lady Helena said. "But in the end,

Mama and I decided you would be the best traveling companion for us."

Faye was ecstatic but tried not to show it. "Thank you. I'm eagerly anticipating the trip."

"We'll give you the particulars shortly. Of course, this is contingent upon your circumstances. If we feel a change renders you unfit, we'll need to find a replacement."

"I don't believe you need to be concerned on that score. I'm sure things will work out."

"And your behavior between now and then must be impeccable."

Faye raised an eyebrow. "I believe my behavior is generally very pleasing."

Lady Helena looked her up and down. "Just making sure we understand one another."

Faye held herself back lest she rendered herself unfit at that very moment.

*****

Faye found Geoff and dragged him towards the hornbeam trees.

He laughed. "What is it?"

She grabbed both his hands and hopped up and down. "I'm going on the trip to Scotland with the Gillinghams!"

He squeezed her hands. "I know how much you wanted to go."

They discussed what few details she had, and then he pulled her down to the ground next to him. "I love this spot. These trees seem so lively and play with the light. And it now has the added distinction of being the place where you agreed to court me."

Though pleasant, she never thought this spot much different from other nice ones in the gardens until the night of the ball. Now it's special to her too.

"I always wished I had the skills to paint this section as I believe it would make a lovely picture." He paused. "Maybe I could get someone to do it with your father's permission."

"I'm sure he'd be delighted to grant that request."

"What would be really fine is if I could get a newer artist. Someone who could use a commission or a chance to be seen. It would be nice to sponsor someone, and they could stay at Yardley while they worked."

"What a wonderful idea. You're continuing your mission to be a patron of the arts."

"Perhaps I'll speak with Mother about it. I think she'd be keen, and she might have other ideas." Geoff grinned. "Aunt Bonnie spoiled us and saved half a blueberry pie if you're ready to retrieve it."

"Clearly, you're her favorite."

"She said Daisy absconded with a cherry one earlier, so it was only fair."

Faye jumped up. "We can fetch the special basket I made for us."

Geoff's eyes twinkled as he rose. "You packed us a lunch? You shouldn't have."

"I should've included honey. It would have been perfect with our treats."

"I can solve that problem if you're willing to go on a short ride."

"Excellent, and we can enjoy our treats along the way."

*****

Faye gave Geoff a questioning look as the phaeton pulled in front of Yardley.

"I promised you honey." He gave her a sunshine grin while handing her out of the vehicle.

"Where are we going?" Faye asked as he pulled her into a section of the house she'd never been in.

"The pantry."

The kitchen staff seemed surprised to see them. Or maybe just her. It appeared Geoff was a regular visitor.

"Mister Geoffrey, it was bad enough when you were coming," a woman chided him. "You really can't bring the ladies down here. Your father will have my hide."

"It's our secret, Molly. Faye won't tell anyone. Right?" He winked at Faye.

She grinned and then nodded.

"We've come for honey," Geoff declared, suddenly looking like a young boy.

Molly looked exasperated but smiled. "You could have sent someone down here for that." She spoke to another girl, who disappeared, and then took the basket from Faye. "Now, would you please return to the drawing room so we can do this properly?"

"Could we eat someplace else?" Faye asked Geoff. "What's your favorite spot?"

"The Galleria is where I read. As long as we don't smear honey all over the family portraits, we should be all right."

Faye giggled.

"I'll spread a blanket or something."

"We can see to that, Mister Geoffrey," Molly chimed in. "Just please, show Miss Faye to the space, and we'll take care of the rest."

"Thank you. You're priceless," said Geoff. "And what treat tonight?"

Molly shook her head and then smiled. "It'll be the last orange ice. On the table like it always is. Don't tell anyone."

"You're good to me." Geoff grabbed Faye's hand and led her out of the kitchen area.

Faye gave a belly laugh. "It seems you have a way with women in charge of food."

Geoff chuckled. "Molly has been with us since I was a young lad, and she a young woman. We're fortunate that turnover at Yardley is low." He paused. "Do you like what you're seeing now?"

Faye beamed at him. "Yes, very much so."

He stopped short and then gave her the swiftest kiss. "Good. This way."

Faye stared at him open-mouthed as he walked ahead of her. It was so quick that she thought she'd dreamt it.

He smiled and held out his hand. "Come on then."

She giggled as she took it, and the two made their way to the Galleria.

*****

Geoff

Geoff had chickened out at the last moment, so it was barely a kiss, but he'd done it, and it had registered. He could see it all over her face. She was shocked, but didn't seem at all displeased. Geoff felt like puffing his chest out, rooster-like.

"Have you ever seen a honeycomb close up?" he asked.

Faye shook her head.

"Then let's take a detour before we go to the Galleria."

Instead of heading upstairs, Geoff led Faye towards the doors at the end of the hall, where he grabbed a long coat, some gloves, and a mask with netting that hung on a nearby hook. They ambled through several garden sections to a few beehives.

"Wait here, please." Geoff put his gear on as he walked towards the hives. He carefully pulled a shelf and, standing absolutely still, gave the bees a few moments to fly off.

Faye gaped at him when he walked back to her. "You keep bees?"

"Yes." He showed her the shelf. "I marvel at the design. These are amazingly complex but still extraordinarily simple."

"How did I not know you do this?"

"It's not a subject that comes up much in conversation."

"But if it's important to you, I'd want to know of it."

Geoff's heart swelled.

"Isn't this something an elderly parson would do?"

Geoff chuckled. "When Clive came home from university during his first summer recess and found out, he teased me mercilessly for a while."

"I like you in this pursuit, for it seems in keeping with your personality. How long have you been doing this?"

"Seven or eight years."

"That's about as long as I've been sculpting."

"I began just after you left for school in London."

"You remember the exact timing so clearly as that?"

He paused. "Your departure was disappointing for me." That event was when he first realized he was partial towards her.

"Oh." Her cheeks turned rosy.

"That along with the dissolution of a false friendship, the bees were a welcome diversion."

"I'm sorry to hear that, Geoff."

He shrugged. "They dropped me for Clive when they heard he was the heir. I've grown used to that sort of behavior by now, but that was the first real incident, and it threw me."

"I can't imagine anyone treating you in such a manner. Despite being a private man, you're usually very honest." She bit her lip. "I think that's why your offer to court me to trick Clive surprised me so. It seemed out of character for you."

"It might have been in a way, but my offer wasn't as deceptive as you may believe."

Faye studied him for a moment. "What's the appeal with the bees?"

"Honey is quite tasty."

Faye smiled. "But why not buy it? Isn't this extraordinarily difficult?"

"It does take a great deal of care. Too many who have hives end up killing many of the bees. I'm trying to employ the hive designs I've read about, so all the bees live."

"That's lovely and sounds just like you. You said you had no occupation."

"This is something, but I'd consider it more an avocation than a serious pursuit. It's nothing on the level of your sculpting."

"I think it's wonderful. I'm sure you could make all kinds of things. Speaking of, do you think they've brought the honey up by now?"

"Most likely. Let's go eat."

*****

They entered the Galleria, and Faye stopped short. "Gracious," she whispered.

"You've never been up here?" he asked, surprised.

Faye shook her head.

"That seems so odd as often as you've been here," Geoff commented. "Scores of strangers tour through here every year."

"I would've been with Clive much of the time, and I can't imagine this is a space in which he spends his afternoons." Faye walked towards a portrait of the brothers. Clive had his arm around Geoff, and they appeared to be about ten and twelve years of age, maybe a year or two before she'd met them. "What a charming portrait. You two were such cute boys."

Despondency settled over Geoff. "Yes, we were."

Faye took his hand. "What's troubling you? What's wrong with you and Clive?"

How can I tell her? I barely know what's wrong with me.

"I hope it's not me," she said quietly.

Geoff pulled her close. "You may have been the spark, but the powder keg has been there for a while." He kissed the top of her head. "It's not you. It's me. It's him. And I can barely put into words what's wrong. Everything is all tossed up right now, and I don't know how to set it aright again."

Faye wrapped her arms around him.

"I'm sorry we've put you in an unfair position," Geoff said.

"I'm so happy you asked to court me. You weren't joking about liking me, were you?"

"I'd never been more serious in my life."

"So this was real for you?"

"Very much so."

"It must have killed you to hear me jabber on and on about Clive."

Geoff gave a half-hearted laugh. "It got tiresome, yes."

Faye winced. "I'm sorry. I'm complaining about Clive not seeing me, and I did the same thing to you."

"Clive is Clive. And I am... Geoff."

"Yes. I almost missed something very good if you hadn't taken the first step. I only see and think of you now, Geoff."

He couldn't breathe. *Faye Armstrong wants me?*

She giggled. "Yes, you. The question was written all over your face."

"Then you know how thrilled I am to hear that." He cleared his throat. "I think I found our snack."

It was an excellent tray arrangement with Geoff's honey, Faye's basket and contents, plus a few extras.

"Before we dive in, do you think you could..." Faye's cheeks turned pink. "That kiss was so quick, I wondered if it had happened. Do you think you could..."

Geoff beamed. "Absolutely."

He leaned over.

"Make sure it's longer this time."

He chuckled. "As you wish, Miss Faye."

And longer it was.

CHAPTER 17

The Ball at Hartwell

Geoff

FAYE AND GEOFF ENTERED the ballroom at Hartwell. It was the last day of August, and the first large social event Jarvis and Mariah would host since he inherited the dukedom. Many guests of nobility and land-owning families traveled to be in attendance tonight.

Tonight was the first time Geoff and Faye attended an important social event as a courting couple. A potential marriage alliance was important for his family, and he wanted Faye introduced properly.

Lord Thurston was in attendance and introduced Geoff, Faye, and Clive to his good friends, Lord and Lady Darton.

"How are you getting on with the architect?" Lord Darton asked Geoff.

"Well. Lord Vaughnryd selected one of the plans, and we're working out arrangements for the surveying." Geoff consulted with the same architect Lord Darton used for his residences in Bath.

"Have you been cornered by Mr. Yeatman yet?" Clive asked Lord Thurston.

"I'm trying to avoid him." Lord Thurston threw back some punch as Jarvis walked up beside him. "Did you have to invite him?"

"The biggest shipper and one of the richest men in the country?" the duke replied. "Need you ask?"

"I was hoping to enjoy myself tonight."

"There's a pretty lady who's been eyeing you like cake," Clive remarked.

"Another person I'm trying to avoid." Lord Thurston laid his empty glass on the tray and took another. "Did you really have to invite the Beaumont siblings?"

"If Lady Edith Beaumont glares at me any harder, you may need the magistrate," said Lady Darton.

Jarvis shook his head. "I can't not invite the only other marquess my age."

"I suppose," agreed Lord Thurston. "Though Lord Kengsley makes my skin crawl."

"I second that," Lady Darton said.

"Is he another person you're hiding from, Lord Thurston?" Geoff asked wryly.

Faye chuckled.

"It's becoming a large club," said Lord Darton. "By the way, my mother is in attendance and inquired after you, Thurston."

He shuddered. "That woman is terrifying. What would be grand is if you could put them all in the same room, Jarvis."

"Do you think we could introduce Lady Helena to Lord Kengsley while they're in that room?" asked Clive.

Geoff rolled his eyes. "You fellows gossip worse than the elderly ladies in the village."

"You're right. Enough gossip," declared Jarvis. "Lady Darton, your numbers for the silk mill are genius—"

"I'm not discussing business tonight."

"But I thought you loved numbers?" Jarvis smirked.

Lady Darton gave him a look. "Speaking of love, maybe the next Duchess of Hartwell is here tonight. Do you wish me to find Lady Helena?"

"I believe she was speaking with Lady Edith," Jarvis replied. "Perhaps the four of us can find that room Lord Thurston mentioned and chat."

Lady Darton pointed a finger at him.

Her husband threw his hands out. "You're like children. We're at a ball, for heaven's sake. Don't you have some guests to mingle with, Duke Hartwell?"

"Kicked out of my conversation at my own ball. I'm mingling with the lot of you. You're guests and the most entertaining bunch here," Jarvis responded lightly. "Fine. I'll be a proper host and mingle. Spalding? Thurston? Are you with me? I think Mariah invited some of her lady friends tonight if you're interested."

"I am," answered Clive, "But I clearly remember you swearing off women."

Lord Thurston smirked. "How's that working for you, Jarvis?"

"Very well, thank you, and I'm still standing by being married to my pursuits," Jarvis answered. "I'm doing this for the two of you."

Faye was still chuckling as Jarvis, Clive, and Lord Thurston walked off. "Your new business associates are rather singular," she said to Geoff.

"I'll have to thank Clive later."

"How are you surviving the windstorm that is Duke Hartwell?" Lord Darton asked.

"I've known him since we were children, so I'm not a stranger to being dumped in unknown territory," Geoff responded.

"I heard he tried to corner you into a project, Miss Armstrong," Lady Darton said.

Faye was surprised. "He did, but I don't believe that'll work out."

"He'll find a way," Lord Darton said.

"So you're good with numbers, Lady Darton?" Faye asked.

"My wife is a gifted mathematician and astronomer," Lord Darton replied with pride. "She published a paper several months ago."

"How remarkable!" Faye exclaimed.

"I do like numbers, yes," Lady Darton said. "I made the mistake of telling Duke Hartwell I could use them to help him in his business."

They spoke with Lord and Lady Darton for a while longer, and then the two pairs separated.

Geoff and Faye spoke with a few people closer to his parent's age. He particularly enjoyed talking with one gentleman and his wife, whose family bred horses.

He introduced Faye to another couple, who exchanged the quickest of looks as he did so.

"Miss Faye," the wife said coolly. "You're much more genteel than I expected."

Geoff was about to give a retort when he felt the slightest pressure on his arm from Faye.

"My aunts are very accomplished and made sure my cousin, Miss Caldwell, and myself received excellent tutoring and schooling," Faye replied.

How did she keep her tone so in check?

"Yes, Mrs. Caldwell is an excellent woman. You were fortunate to have such a person take you on."

"I do consider myself the most fortunate of girls to call her aunt. My family is tremendous." She glanced at Geoff. "Would you mind terribly if we got some refreshment? I am so thirsty."

"Not at all. If you will excuse us," Geoff said a little shortly to the couple. He exhaled as they walked away. "I admire how ladylike you act when the situation can test you, but it's a wonder you can let people speak to you in such a fashion."

"I address the most egregious displays, but let other offenses go, so I don't become bitter. It's not like everyone I meet and know is of the same mind; you being case and point."

"You need never doubt my regard for you," he said softly.

*****

Geoff and Faye were discussing other topics when he spotted Mr. Nash Repington. Geoff had met Repington the previous fall at a hunting house gathering and had enjoyed his light-hearted demeanor. The gentleman quickly came their way.

"Fitz!" Repington exclaimed and gave him a hearty handshake.

Geoff introduced Faye, and they exchanged pleasantries. Then Faye excused herself so the men could catch up with one another.

"Very nice, Fitz," commented Repington. "Is she the one you spoke of during our stay at Stoddard Grove?"

"She is indeed."

"And how successful have you been at wresting her affections from your clueless brother? She seems very much inclined towards you."

"We're courting." Geoff grinned.

"Excellent! Did Spalding not care or notice?"

"He noticed." Geoff paused. "There's been no blatant interference thus far, but there are indications he'll not ignore it."

Repington was quiet a moment. "I'd carefully consider taking that stance with him. Miss Armstrong is certainly a beauty, but there are other ladies, and you'd have little trouble getting one to court you."

"But not the one I want."

"Ironic, isn't it?"

"Thank you for your concern, but it's done and without regret. We'll see where it leads."

"You care for her a great deal then?" Repington asked.

"I do. I have for quite some time."

"I hope to become better acquainted with Miss Armstrong."

The two men spoke for a while.

Repington pointed. "Is that a cause for concern?"

Geoff watched Faye dance with Clive. Ordinarily, such a sight would be normal and quite proper since the man in question was his brother. But he knew how Faye felt about Clive once, and he definitely knew Clive.

"I'm sure it's fine," Geoff replied. "But perhaps I'll make myself readily available for the next dance."

The two parted.

She's spent time with me privately and said she only saw and thought of me now. But Geoff still had a hard time shaking off his unease.

Faye and Clive finished their dance, and a few moments later, Faye walked towards Geoff, her smile fading as she drew near. "What's the matter?"

He forced a grin. "Would you favor me with a dance now?"

Faye beamed and took his hand. "Nothing would make me happier."

Geoff led her to the floor, trying to forget the dance she had prior.

✳✳✳✳✳

Faye

Faye loved Geoff's attention, and she was delighted to be on his arm throughout the evening. After growing used to the idea of courting him with the intention of marriage, Faye wasn't blind to what that meant socially. She would move in slightly higher circles than she was accustomed, and her comportment must be impeccable.

Geoff had lost some of his earlier energy. She wouldn't be surprised if he was slowly growing tired of being here, but it felt more deeply rooted than his normal disinclination towards large social gatherings. He seemed disturbed. "Are you sure you're all right?"

"I apologize. I'm just out of sorts tonight."

He hadn't been out of sorts earlier, more the opposite. "Is there anything I can do?"

He paused.

"Geoff?" she prompted. He really was acting oddly. "Something is bothering you, and you don't want to tell me."

"It shouldn't bother me."

"Even if it shouldn't, you can share with me. Perhaps it'll ease your mind."

He studied her for a moment. "Did you enjoy your dance with Clive?"

Her steps faltered. *Oh.* "I did. Is that what's troubling you?"

He looked away.

Faye was at a loss. "I thought nothing of it. It seemed perfectly natural that he'd ask."

"Of course." He didn't sound like he meant the words.

"I told you before I cared only for you," she said in a low voice. "Why are you in doubt?"

"I don't know. But you were enamored with him before."

"And now I'm enamored with you."

"But it happened quickly. It might be difficult to completely and truly transfer your affections."

Faye stopped dancing. "Are you calling me fickle?"

Geoff's eyes widened. "No, of course not."

They resumed dancing, but Faye's steps were more rigid. "You believe Clive could sway me back with just one dance?"

Geoff opened and shut his mouth.

Faye stopped again and glared at him. "You did!"

"It's not so much swayed back; it's more how anchored your feelings were to begin with."

She gasped and then marched off the dance floor into the hall area.

"Faye!" Geoff rushed after her.

"I can't believe you!" She tried to keep her voice down, but she felt like yelling.

"I know how Clive is."

"Maybe so, but more importantly, you seem to believe me weak in mind and even weaker in heart. Are you so unable to trust another?"

Geoff's eyes hardened. "Frankly, you haven't given me a ton of evidence for placing trust in our courtship."

Faye's jaw dropped.

"You've been caught up with my brother for an age, and then in a comparatively brief span, would try to convince me with a declaration and a couple of kisses that you've transferred that affection to me."

Faye's temperature rose sharply. "That declaration you've taken so lightly was made with every ounce of sincerity. And as for having a courtship you can't place trust in, that's your fault. It was your idea to begin one based on a sham."

Faye turned on her heel and strode out of the hall.

CHAPTER 18

Can't Continue

Faye

FAYE HADN'T SPOKEN, written, or seen Geoff since their fight a week prior.

It was torture.

She couldn't believe how quickly Geoff had become a central piece of the fabric of her life.

He was here at this Venetian breakfast a neighbor was hosting.

And so was Clive.

Faye and Geoff tried to act like nothing was amiss, but it was difficult. It was even more problematic because Clive was paying her more attention than usual. More attention than most of the other ladies. And definitely more than Lady Helena.

She glared at Faye from a corner.

I'm sinking in quagmire.

"My brother should be more attached to a suitor such as yourself," Clive said. "You could easily get snatched away."

"Perhaps he would, if you were more sparse," Faye remarked wryly.

"You're the best company here. And maybe it's not so evident that he's the one you truly want to be with."

Faye looked away. She was upset with Geoff, but that didn't mean her affections for him had dimmed.

Though he believed her affections weren't that strong to begin with.

Am I fickle? Do I not care for Geoff as strongly as I ought?

"What I wouldn't give to know what you're thinking right now."

Faye shot up from her seat. Clive was playing mind games with her, and he knew her well enough to be effective. "Perhaps you should see to someone else's needs."

Without waiting for a reply, Faye headed towards Geoff and was intercepted by Lady Helena.

"Remember the terms — exceptional behavior, and you can be replaced." She walked off.

Faye rubbed her forehead and then stood next to Geoff.

"Finally, tore yourself from Clive?" he asked dryly.

"There weren't too many other choices since you've made yourself so scarce."

They stood in silence.

Geoff exhaled. "We can't continue like this."

"You're ending our courtship?" she whispered frantically.

"No." He paused. "Unless you wish to?"

Faye shook her head.

Geoff grabbed her hand and led her out of the room.

*****

Geoff

Geoff led Faye outside to the patio. The last thing he wanted to do was pain her, but he couldn't just dismiss his unease either. "I don't know what to do. I don't know how not to doubt."

Faye narrowed her eyes. "I wouldn't lie to you. Especially on a matter so important as this."

"Of course, but I also know how deeply I care for you and how hard it would be to move me off that."

Faye crossed her arms. "So we're back to how fickle I am. Or maybe it's that I'm shallow."

Geoff set his jaw. "Call it what you like. But the depth of your feelings for my brother and me are real issues, and ones which I believe I'm entitled to consider."

Faye's eyes flashed for a second before they cooled, and she cast them downward.

Geoff exhaled. "You've been open the entire time and have done nothing for me to doubt your affection," he acknowledged. "I just do. I can't explain it."

"Probably because I entered this courtship intending to court another. It's natural for you to need even more assurance than my word."

"I know you, Faye. If you spoke it, you meant it."

"That's your rational mind speaking, which doesn't necessarily secure your feelings." Faye peered up at him. "And I want those to be secure as well."

"I appreciate that." Geoff rubbed his face. "My issues with Clive are more a problem than anything."

"It doesn't say much for me to use one brother to make the other jealous." She took a deep breath. "Please believe me when I say you're all I see and think of, even more so now. Clive is my good friend, but you are that and so much more."

He took her hands in his. "And you for me."

Faye kissed his cheek. "Grandfather Sabo is to stay with us in a couple weeks' time. Would you come for dinner the day he arrives and meet him? I'd like for you two to become well acquainted."

Geoff's heart swelled. He knew what her grandfather meant to her. "Of course."

CHAPTER 19

A Boutique

Geoff

JARVIS WAS AT SPALDING for a brief stay and had requested that Geoff and Faye meet with him and Clive. It was the end of September, and Geoff thought it would be an excellent opportunity to update him on the expansion thus far with Lord Vaughnryd. Progress was slow but steady, which pleased Geoff.

"Only two looms?" Jarvis asked Geoff.

He nodded. "I put the order in through you."

"I thought that was just a starting point. I didn't realize this would be the extent of the expansion."

"Lord Vaughnryd and I think it best for now. They've begun surveying the land for the addition to the existing mill. The actual construction may be quicker than usual since the design will be simple and the building materials are nearby. But we want to get an idea for how these machines will change the existing operations before jumping in any farther."

"I was thinking more."

Geoff remained silent. He wasn't budging on this point, and he was sure Lord Vaughnryd would be firm as well.

"People need to know I mean business," said Jarvis.

"And you will lose Lord Vaughnryd's if you push this."

Jarvis sighed. "Point taken. I actually wished for you to view the plans and pictures for the new shop."

"I thought that was being tabled," Clive replied.

"It was, but I sent an inquiry to Lord Darton, and he can put me in touch with people who could turn some of the space into a storefront without too much finagling."

Clive gave Geoff an uneasy glance. "Richard, I wish you'd slow down with this."

"I only wanted to know the possibilities," Jarvis responded. "This will give Fitz more time to think about it."

"I informed you I'm not running a store," Geoff said tightly.

"You don't have to be physically present," Jarvis said. "You can hire other people to do the work—"

"No," Geoff cut in. "And that's the last word we're to have on this subject, Duke Hartwell."

An uneasy silence blanketed the room.

Jarvis cleared his throat and looked towards Faye. "I spoke with my sister about having you do a sculpture of her."

"Thank you for giving me such a distinction," Faye said. "At present, I'm already obligated on two commissions, but I'll be able to begin in a few months."

"Surely Geoff could wait for his piece," Jarvis said. "And he can handle scheduling commissions."

"Why would I do that?" Geoff asked. "I know little of the business of sculpting, and what I do know was furnished by Miss Faye."

"I understand, but once supplied with the facts, you could make the decisions."

Geoff's jaw dropped, and then his eyes narrowed. "We may be friends and you a higher rank, but I grow tired—"

Faye laid a hand on his arm.

*****

Faye

Faye tried to communicate silently that Geoff didn't have to go charging in on her behalf just yet, though she valued how readily he fought for her welfare and dignity.

If Duke Hartwell wished, he could have communicated solely to her through Geoff or even her father, as most other gentlemen would. The fact he had not and asked for her presence with the other men said something, though Faye wasn't entirely sure what.

"I appreciate your eagerness to include me, Duke Hartwell," Faye said. "However, it's best if I schedule my own commissions since I'm most knowledgeable in that arena, and I'd be more comfortable if I could speak with Lady Mariah myself."

"We could probably call on her tomorrow if you're available," Duke Hartwell offered.

"You just arrived here," Geoff said incredulously.

Duke Hartwell shrugged. "I'll take Clive back with me. He can visit me at Hartwell as easily as I can him at Spalding."

Clive nodded. "True enough."

Geoff sighed. "Miss Faye and I have an important dinner engagement this evening. Would another day suit?"

"Certainly. Just let me know, and I'll work it out with my sister."

CHAPTER 20

Grandfather Sabo

Geoff

GEOFF WAS NERVOUS as he stood on the front porch of Oakes Hollow, waiting for the doorman to answer. He felt this dinner would be critical. Even though Faye knew her own mind, her grandfather's opinions mattered greatly. His disapproval could make an already challenging courtship more so.

Geoff thought himself open-minded, so he was embarrassed to admit his surprise at the personage of Mr. George Sabo when introduced, despite everything he'd heard about him. Mr. Sabo was tall, slender, and dark-skinned, a handsome gentleman with strong cheekbones and jawline. His countenance was initially serious and penetrating until he offered a warm and friendly smile.

Geoff liked him immediately.

He shook Mr. Sabo's large, calloused hand. Firm grip — Geoff liked that too.

"I wanted to meet the gentleman Wyatt praised so high in his letters." Mr. Sabo's quiet, bass voice reverberated in the drawing room. "For a while, I feared Faye would never marry, for surely her father would never find a man good enough for his princess."

Faye chuckled and squeezed Geoff's arm. "Grandpapa."

"Mr. Fitzpatrick, would you favor me with a walk?" Mr. Sabo asked. "Touring the grounds is one of my highlights when I visit."

"Certainly, sir."

"Thank you."

"You waste no time, Father." Mr. Armstrong clapped Geoff's shoulder. "Don't let him fool you. Father is a gentle chap."

Mr. Sabo gave him a look.

"Sorry, that was supposed to be a secret." Mr. Armstrong winked. "You'll be fine. He let me marry his daughter."

"There was no man of our acquaintance who drooled and doted on her the way he did. It was almost embarrassing." He chuckled, his deep laugh making Geoff smile.

"I don't intend to keep you from Faye long," Mr. Sabo said once they were outside. "My favorite part of the gardens is the hornbeam trees."

"That's my favorite spot as well."

"And what do you like about them?"

"Their character."

Mr. Sabo gave him a curious look.

Geoff felt like a silly schoolboy. "They seem different from the other trees and each other. I could give each of them a name and a story. They make that section of the garden appear a whimsy tale."

Mr. Sabo was quiet.

"I rarely speak in such a manner," Geoff commented. "I'm not usually prone to fancy."

"On the contrary. Your comments speak to a mind that views his reality differently than most and un-apologetically expresses it when you wish." Mr. Sabo stopped walking and turned towards him. "I'm pleased you chose to engage me in a manner different from others of your acquaintance."

"Thank you. May I ask why you like the hornbeams so much?"

Mr. Sabo gazed towards them. "They're tall and strong. Practical and comely. They simply exude the qualities I wish to possess and display. Including the ones you described, perhaps, even more so. The value of a name and story is one some take for granted."

"Faye told me about your family history. She's very proud of it, as she should be."

"Indeed." He paused. "How far back can you trace your histories, Mr. Fitzpatrick?"

"Several hundred years on my father's side. Less on my mother's, but I'd say a few hundred."

"Treasure that. My histories begin with me, for I have scant knowledge of where I actually came from. Just a few hazy memories."

"But your name..." Geoff faltered.

"My first name was given by those who bought me. I selected a surname based on research. It's used in the area of the continent where I might have been born based on shipping manifests." Mr. Sabo began walking again. "Lord Vaughnryd told me you're working with him on his mill."

"I am." Geoff rushed to catch up, surprised at the abrupt change in subject. He was still digesting what Mr. Sabo had just shared.

"Do you enjoy that work?"

Geoff was quiet for a second. As much as he wanted to be found pleasing by Faye's grandfather, that question touched on personal challenges of his, and he didn't generally divulge those. But he suspected Mr. Sabo had just related matters extremely close to him, and so Geoff felt more inclined to act in like manner. "I'm unsure if I wish to be busy in that pursuit though I am seeking one. My family is in banking and investment, and I seem to do that well, but again it's not something I particularly enjoy."

"I can sympathize and feel similarly with my business. It's not a love, but it was the best way to provide the type of living I believed me and mine deserved."

"What would you rather be doing, if I may ask?"

"I like rocks."

Geoff stared at him a moment and then laughed.

"I believe that's why Lord Vaughnryd and I get along so well together," Mr. Sabo said. "Only he enjoys building things, and I'm fascinated with their actual composition."

"Faye enjoys turning them into wonderful pieces of art."

"I never thought of it in that vein, but yes, that's true." Mr. Sabo clapped his hands. "Shall we go back in? Wyatt keeps threatening to defeat me in a game of chess."

✲✲✲✲✲

Faye

After dinner, Geoff, Papa, and Grandfather Sabo had spent some time in the gentlemen's room but then joined everyone in the drawing room.

It's like they've known each other forever.

"It's unusual for you to open up so quickly," she said to Geoff as they sat on the window seat.

"Your grandfather is easy to be comfortable with." He paused. "And I made an effort to be so. I know how important he is to you, and that's important to me."

Faye smiled and squeezed his hand. "Thank you."

The two watched the Armstrong family and her grandfather.

I'm falling hard for him, but has his regard for me grown since we began courting? I've been such a silly girl about Clive until recently, and I don't feel like I've given Geoff much reason to strengthen his attachment. Does he seriously view me as a wife? Was it ever Geoff's intention to marry me?

"What is it, Faye?" Geoff asked. "You were so gladsome, and now you look miserable."

"Perhaps I'm overtired." *There's no 'perhaps' about it. I feel exhausted.*

*****

Geoff

Something is very wrong.

Geoff pulled Faye from the window seat and led her through the drawing room's exterior doors. After grabbing a lantern from a post, they continued towards the hornbeam trees.

He stopped walking, set the lantern on a nearby rock, and peered at her. "I won't force you to confide in me," he said gently. "But please give me the chance to help if I can. It's seldom I see you so distressed."

Faye started playing with her hands. "Do you actually want to be married one day?"

Geoff looked amused. "Yes. Courting you wouldn't make much sense if I didn't."

"Some do it for just amusement."

"I never viewed courtship as diverting entertainment." He chuckled. "Girls tended to confuse and, on some levels, scare me."

"Oh."

"Not you, of course. That's probably why I care for you so much." He gave one of her curls an affectionate tug.

She flushed. "I feel like such a goose now. Here I'm worrying you might not care for me as much as I do you."

"Why would you think that?"

Faye glanced away. "Clive has such a commanding presence, doesn't he?"

Geoff studied her. "What are you saying?"

"I was afraid your stronger motivation for this relationship was still getting at him. Not that you don't care for me, just that priority-wise, if there was a choice between hurting Clive or us..."

"That was never a contest, Faye. The goal was always you. Clive was just an impediment."

"Oh." Faye played with her hands.

"I have my difficulties with Clive, but he's my brother, and I still love him as such."

"Of course. I didn't mean to imply that you meant him actual harm." Faye bit her lip. "But the anger and resentment are real, Geoff. You two need to resolve that before you reach a place from which you can't return."

Geoff exhaled. "I know." He gave her a rueful smile. "Did this conversation ease your mind at all or just increase your anxiety?"

"It was good we had it. I know your goals and wishes."

"Was that explanation better than a marriage proposal?"

Faye gave a nervous giggle. "Yes. I mean, I wanted to know if that was your goal, but I'm not quite ready to accept yet."

Geoff took her hand. "That's fine."

"But you would have asked if you thought I was?"

Geoff contemplated that. "I'm not sure."

Faye stared at him a moment. "Are you still unsure of me?"

He hesitated. "No."

Faye bit her lip.

Geoff took her other hand and gave them both a gentle squeeze. "No," he repeated more firmly. "And I think we're just the right speed for one another."

CHAPTER 21

The Hands of Lady Mariah

Faye

FAYE REPLAYED HER CONVERSATION with Geoff as the carriage took her to Hartwell the first week in October. They seemed well but tentative. *Our courtship would be perfect if it hadn't begun predicated on a farce. I'm not sure what's real and not, despite Geoff's assurances and mine.*

Geoff had offered to escort her, but Faye had told him she wanted to do this visit on her own as a commission from a duke for his sister duchess was of great importance, and so requested that her father's steward accompany her for the two days. However, their situation might have been the larger reason for declining his escort, for she wanted some time apart to think.

Lady Mariah shut the door to her private sitting room after Faye entered. "I'm so pleased you came to see me about this. The men can't do anything, can they?"

Faye chuckled. "I believe Geoff and Lord Vaughnryd are working well together, but things seem a bit of a shambles where I come in."

"Now, if I have this correct, my energetic brother wishes me to have a sculpture done by you that will eventually model a dress, wrap, or some sort of apparel?"

"Yes, that is his idea."

"A sculpture of myself feels pretentious. Do you paint or draw?"

"I don't paint well at all. I'm better at sketching and drawing, but sculpting is by far my forte." Faye paused. "I don't have to do your whole person. A small portion of you, like your hands, could be provocative. Your fingers are very long, slender, and graceful, and would make a lovely composition. I always thought I had childlike hands."

"I like that idea. And they could hold a wrap or scarf?"

Faye nodded.

"But I believe Richard was hoping for instant recognition," Lady Mariah remarked.

"I believe a sign stating 'the hands of Lady Mariah' would do just as well or even better. He's attempting to sell the cloth, not you. An overdone statue might take attention away from the true goal."

"Perfect. And when he's done with it, the hands shall be mine?"

"Yes, they'll be yours to do what you wish."

Lady Mariah clapped. "Now I'm actually excited about this. Tell me how we are to proceed."

"I can do sketches of your hands during my stay now, but I'm afraid I won't be able to begin the sculpting yet. I already have two commissions and an upcoming trip."

"And a possible marriage."

Faye flushed with heat. "I believe your brother hoped I'd get it done sooner rather than later."

"That sounds just like him. He's too used to getting his way. I hope you held your ground."

"In a manner of speaking."

"Good. You're far too busy with previous engagements. He's fortunate you're giving this consideration at all. I'll speak with him. He's so impatient."

*****

Faye hoped beginning the rough sketches might placate Duke Hartwell since she couldn't do the actual sculpture for some time. She suggested Lady Mariah engage in a series of activities using her hands, so the duchess began with needlepoint and then moved on to writing a letter.

"How are you and Geoff?" Lady Mariah grinned.

Faye couldn't help a small smile. "We hit a little rough patch, but we seem to be on firmer ground again."

"Good. He's completely besotted with you. I'm glad he was finally forward."

"You knew before he asked?"

"Yes, I encouraged him to be more forthright. I love his quietness, but it makes it a bit of a challenge to communicate, doesn't it?"

"Yes, it does."

It never occurred to Faye that the duchess would be so interested, on a personal level, in her and Geoff's courtship. Not that Faye had any intentions of botching things, but that increased the pressure for her courtship to progress well.

"I rather wonder that you're not currently married," Faye commented tentatively. That was forward, given their acquaintance, and she only dared mention it because the duchess had been involved in her own courtship behind the scenes.

"Marriage is a serious endeavor, isn't it?" Lady Mariah sighed. "It's difficult to know if a man is truly about you sometimes."

"I can imagine that must be very challenging given your circumstances."

"I tend to select the wrong men."

"Maybe you should choose the absolute last gentleman you believe would be fitting," Faye joked.

Lady Mariah giggled. "You'd have me marry a rake or a ruffian?"

"Not exactly, just the last man of your acquaintance whom you would ever consider."

"That would probably be Lord Spalding."

Faye was taken aback. "He was the last name I expected to hear."

"No offense to your taste in gentlemen, but I find him rather vapid."

Faye raised an eyebrow.

"That might be severe," Lady Mariah admitted. "But it's as though everything was handed to him on a silver platter, and he bounces along without a care. I just wish him to be more serious."

It was those qualities that had probably drawn Faye to him, but in the end, she'd chosen the more sober brother. "Do you believe me serious and steady of purpose?"

"I suppose serious isn't the first adjective that comes to mind, but you're certainly not silly. And anyone who can complete sculpture commissions must be steady of purpose."

I won't divulge I haven't completed one yet.

CHAPTER 22

Wingman

Geoff

CURIOUS, GEOFF ENTERED the drawing room. A visit from Jarvis was always welcome, but it wasn't as though he lived close enough to just call. He must have traveled with Faye upon her return.

"How do you feel about a journey to Bath?" Jarvis inquired with no preamble.

Geoff stared at him for a moment. "Ambivalent."

"That's good enough for me. Clive won't accompany me to see Lord Broughton."

"And you believe I'll be more inclined?"

"You're actually the better person since you're more involved and helping Lord Vaughnryd. You can speak sensibly about the operations."

Geoff held back a frown. *I'm more involved than Clive? How did that happen?*

"It's an actual appointment," Jarvis pressed. "He agreed to a meeting."

"I must confess I didn't expect that."

"No matter what Udayle told him, old Lord Broughton probably knows a good thing when he hears it. A behemoth like him shouldn't be hard to get in line."

Geoff frowned. "They were massive, powerful creatures, and Lord Broughton is not ancient. I'd imagine he'll be harder to move than you anticipate, and probably for good reason."

"These older people are stuck in their ways and resistant to progress."

"Or they discern the disaster. Maybe you should just speak with him about the industry."

"We don't have time for that, and I'd rather strike while things are hot. Can you come?"

"When?"

"Today... ish."

Geoff gaped at him.

"The appointment is next week, so there's a little time, but we need to leave shortly," Jarvis clarified.

Geoff sighed. *Maybe I can learn something from Lord Broughton then.* "Yes, I'll go with you."

CHAPTER 23

The Gathering

Faye

IN TYPICAL FAYE FASHION, she hadn't done anything for her bottom drawer. Aunt Bonnie held back her exasperation, but Faye decided she'd ask Daisy to do some shopping with her for the day.

Given her relationship with Geoff, it should have been an exhilarating excursion. But it still didn't feel quite real, as though she were on the verge of getting engaged and married.

Clive called on her and Daisy the following day.

"I promised you two fun this summer," Clive said. "Autumn is already half done, and I've been woefully remiss."

"Actually, you told us you needed to be a serious businessman," Daisy remarked wryly. "And since we're not on a tropical island, I didn't expect much excitement."

Clive waved a hand. "We can have a good frolic anyway. Geoff is traveling with Jarvis, and I need

some amusement. Are you two game for a get-together?"

"Sounds grand," answered Daisy. "Faye?"

"I have no engagements."

"Excellent. I miss being with you, Faye," Clive said. "You're with my brother all the time now."

Daisy shot him an odd glance.

"That happens when you court someone, Clive."

"But you don't have to abandon your friends. Or are you keeping your distance for other reasons?" He winked.

Faye cleared her throat and looked away.

Clive said goodbye and took off.

"What was that all about?" Daisy asked.

"Nothing. Clive being silly as usual."

"But his silliness rarely upsets you. Did you fancy him at one time?"

Faye bit her lip. "I did, but it's long forgotten."

"Apparently not by him."

*****

Faye was always well amused at Spalding and with Clive, but this get-together differed from the norm. There were only two other gentlemen and ladies, and they paired off immediately. She, Daisy, and Clive could have gone missing for all they knew.

Plus, Clive seemed out of sorts. He was snapping at the servant staff in a manner Faye had never witnessed. While Clive customarily enjoyed drinks with company, he was more inebriated than Faye had ever seen, which concerned her. As did this current Geoff rant in which he was engaged. Faye felt caught in the middle again, and for the first time, wished to leave Spalding early.

Clive scowled. "For someone who doesn't want it, Geoff always gets attention."

Daisy snorted. "He does not garner that much notice. It's usually the Clive show. Are you that threatened on the few occasions he receives a little?"

Clive glared at her.

"Do you really believe he gets that much?" Faye asked.

"He has yours," Clive retorted.

"We've been through this," Faye said. "We're courting. And I'm here with you now."

"Only because he's gone," Clive replied petulantly.

Faye sighed. It was true, but Clive was acting childish.

"The Great Geoff does everything perfectly," Clive sneered.

"I think you need to leave off the wine," Daisy remarked.

"And now he'll get the perfect wife and have the perfect marriage. Tons of money, heirs in spades, and he'll probably have a grand time—"

Daisy snatched his glass. "That's enough for you, mister."

Faye glowered at him as she shot up from her chair. "Daisy, I just recalled something I needed to tend to at home."

The girls headed towards the door.

"You always had more fun with me, Faye," Clive called after them.

Faye made a disgusted sound.

Daisy gave a low whistle after they climbed into their carriage. "That boy is headed for calamity. Make sure he doesn't take you with him."

"Whatever do you mean?"

"I admire the closeness you two share, but I don't think he's always the most positive influence on you." Daisy patted Faye's leg. "I'm glad you chose Geoff."

Faye bit her lip. "Do you think I'm good for Geoff?"

"Of course! You pull him out of his shell, and he needs that."

But I pitted one brother against the other to get what I wanted, which didn't even turn out to be what I wanted, and now look at the mess that's been created. Geoff shouldn't be with such a selfish creature. I probably deserve a disaster like Clive.

Daisy rubbed her arm. "Faye?"

Faye looked at her with a start.

"What's the matter?" Daisy asked. "Don't let Clive upset you."

"I won't. Let's forget about him and stop in the village for some tea and bread."

*****

The following day, Faye was organizing the items she had bought for her chest when the butler announced Lord Spalding was there to call upon her.

Faye made a face but went to meet him.

He bowed low. "Faye, I was a brute yesterday. Please accept my apology. I don't know what got into me."

"Too much wine," Faye answered wryly.

"Let me make it up to you. I'll take you to London for oysters on Monday."

"That's hardly necessary. Your apology will suffice."

"No, it's not enough. Let me do this for you. I know you love them, and you can name the place."

There were two places she especially liked, and Papa usually took her when they were in London for the season, as a special father-daughter ramble. But she was uncomfortable going with Clive, for this felt suspect. Faye surmised his comments yesterday weren't wholly the result of a drunken rant.

"Let's bring Daisy," Faye suggested. "She suffered through your boorishness as well."

Clive's face fell for a second before he recovered. "Yes, she did. That's a fine idea."

Faye went to tell Daisy after he had left, feeling better about the outing. It would be a delightful day trip to London, and it was nice of Clive to remember.

CHAPTER 24

The Curriculum

Geoff

JARVIS HAD ARRANGED for a private room in a club for gentlemen to meet with Lord Broughton. It was a small space but nicely furnished.

Lord Broughton sighed. "I offer the jennies, and to larger operations, the power looms. They're a good combination for the smaller scale production of many of my clients, and they're reliable."

Jarvis shook his head. "The power loom is wasted on a small scale. We need to go larger — employ more people, bring down costs, sell more product."

"So that the people can become just another machine?" Lord Broughton scowled. "The merchants too in your eyes, I suppose."

"I don't see the workers getting wealthy and having leisure off your jennies system."

"And you're promising them something much better? Duke or no duke, I've been told you're not to be trusted," Lord Broughton commented evenly.

Jarvis made a face. "By Mr. Udayle, no doubt."

"I trust him implicitly. He's a great asset to my millworks."

"If your trust were better placed, you may do better," retorted Jarvis.

"Duke Hartwell," Geoff warned.

Lord Broughton narrowed his eyes. "Brash young man who thinks he knows everything. If you believe you can just waltz into this arena and suddenly change everything, Duke Hartwell, you best reconsider."

"Is that a threat?"

"Consider it my only piece of friendly advice I'll impart. A seasoned veteran to a junior who ought to know when to pay deference to his elders."

Geoff swallowed. "We meant no disrespect, Lord Broughton."

"I know you did not, Mr. Fitzpatrick. Your manner the entire time has been flawless. Perhaps your friend will take a lesson from you."

"I need no lessons," Jarvis asserted coldly. "I'm about to rewrite the curriculum. Hopefully, you're not expelled, Lord Broughton,"

Geoff's eyes widened.

"I'll take that challenge, Duke Hartwell. I bid you good day, gentlemen."

*****

Geoff chased after Jarvis as he stormed out of the building. "Jarvis!"

He kept walking.

Geoff caught up and yanked his arm. "Richard!"

He jerked to a stop.

"What has gotten into you?" Geoff exclaimed. "I've never seen you behave that way towards another, especially your elder."

Jarvis jerked out of his grasp. "Deference," he spat out. "He'll defer us into chaos."

"It's a loom," Geoff said incredulously. "Society will not go down because Lord Broughton didn't sell the latest innovation."

"We should use our advantages to make things better."

"He is in his own way."

"Order and efficiency bring security. He's stuck in the past."

Geoff studied his friend. "Lord Broughton isn't your father, and Hartwell isn't the world."

"But I am the title."

Geoff was quiet for a moment. *Where is this coming from?* "No. You inherited a title. You are Richard Jarvis."

"Fat lot that means," Jarvis muttered as he paced, rubbing his head as he did so. "I don't know what happened to me. It's like I snapped."

"You need to leave this alone for a bit. Take a few weeks' break." Geoff couldn't believe he was about to suggest this. "Why don't we spend a couple of extra days in Bath and stomp around?"

"Truly? You don't really stomp around."

Geoff shrugged. "I'll make an exception in this case."

Jarvis clapped his shoulder. "You're an anchor, Geoff. I'm glad you came with me."

"I'm glad I did too."

"I can't just leave things be, but perhaps you're right. Let's stomp around Bath for a couple of days."

CHAPTER 25

Mind Games

Geoff

GEOFF'S CONVERSATION WITH JARVIS still disturbed him a week later. He was concerned for his friend.

"Do you feel you are the title?" Geoff asked his brother the evening of his return from Bath. "That you're not...Clive?"

"That's a bit deep for this time of night."

Geoff exhaled. "Nevermind."

"What made you ask?"

"Something Jarvis stated."

"He thinks too much."

"That's funny, because I frequently think of Jarvis as impulsive and restless."

"He's that too. The man is a walking contradiction. I'm not the marquess yet."

"I know, but you've been groomed for it all your life, and you're in charge of Spalding as though you were one."

"I've never seen Spalding as a training ground. To me, it's the place where I can live and breathe before I have to be a real nobleman."

Geoff studied his brother. "You feel you can't do that at Yardley?"

"I was happy there when we were young, but as we grew older, it felt more like a responsibility instead of a home."

"But you're at Yardley frequently."

"I'm by myself at Spalding. Unlike you, I actually prefer company."

"I'm not a misanthrope, but I like real companionship, not just a gaggle of persons."

Clive chuckled. "Sometimes the gaggle is entertaining."

"It just makes me irritable."

"I suppose when the gaggle sees me as a walking estate and bag of cash, that does get tiring. It'd be nice to be remembered for something other than a rich nobleman." He gave Geoff a weak smile. "Nice thing about Faye. I am always Clive with her."

Geoff nodded.

"But at the same time, I do enjoy my lot in life." He smirked. "Gloating that you don't have to worry about such things? It's like you get the money without the responsibilities."

Geoff scowled. "I wouldn't gloat over that."

"I keep my expectations low and shallow for myself and others, my close acquaintances few, and then no one is disappointed."

"I'd hardly think you'd be satisfied with that."

Clive jumped up from his chair. "Maybe you don't know me as well as you think, little brother."

*****

Faye and Geoff had planned a ride for the afternoon, and Faye waited in the Galleria at Yardley for him to return from an errand. She had arrived early, and he apparently was running late.

She nervously paced, viewing the fine paintings as she did so. She'd only seen Geoff a couple of times in the three weeks since they'd had their last serious discussion about their relationship, the day he met Grandfather Sabo. They hadn't been together this infrequently since their courtship began.

Faye was admiring an older family portrait when Clive walked through, and she jumped.

"I'd wondered where you'd gotten to," Clive remarked. "You weren't in your usual spots." His face clouded over. "This is usually Geoff's space."

"Yes, I figured it'd be a suitable place to wait for him."

"I wager you're expecting a proposal any day now."

"I suspect it's a little ways off."

"Geoff returning to his shell?"

Faye glared at him.

Clive raised his hands in defense. "Proposing is a monumental event for most gentlemen. For a man like Geoff, he might pass out during the process."

"Yes, because marriage to me would be dreadful," Faye said wryly. "You've already described your feelings on that subject."

"I never said that, Faye. As a matter of fact, I expressed the opposite not too long ago."

Faye scoffed. "When you had too much to drink."

"I've never questioned your fine qualities or doubted you'd make an excellent wife."

Then why didn't you see me, Clive? Faye shook her head. "Just because Geoff is quiet doesn't mean he has no backbone. He was quite forward when he asked to court me."

"Are you absolutely sure it's Geoff? I had heard you liked me for a while, and then suddenly you're in love with Geoff? Doesn't that seem strange?"

"It was quick," Faye admitted. "But it's not like I haven't known him just as long."

"But as well?"

Faye wavered. "Not at first. But once he let me in, yes, I think I know him just as well."

Clive stepped in closer. "Are you sure, Faye?"

Faye swallowed. *Of course, I'm sure.*

"We were always better friends," said Clive.

"Things change."

"Do they?" He leaned over. "Are you sure Geoff isn't still trying to get at me?"

He might be, but his affection for me is genuine. I know that.

"Are you sure you're completely over me?" Clive asked, his face very close to hers. "It'd be unfair to Geoff to still have feelings for me. You better be sure."

That's true.

"Did they really change, Faye?" Clive's head lowered towards hers, and Faye closed her eyes.

She heard a sound and yanked herself from Clive.

Geoff stood in the hall, white like snow, as a deafening silence filled the room, suffocating Faye. He turned on his heel and fled.

"What were you thinking?" she shouted at Clive.

"I didn't hear any complaints from your end," he yelled back.

Faye growled and then took off, with Clive fast on her heels.

"How could you make me do this to him?" she cried.

"Make you? I didn't force you to do anything!"

"You were playing mind games."

"Like what you two were playing?"

Faye faltered. She'd never felt more shame in her life. "We killed him, Clive. It's like I'm tied to you in some sick way."

"Yeah, I know," he said in a twisted voice. "I'm never as good as the Great Geoff."

"What's going on?" Lady Yardley asked in a firm voice at the bottom of the steps.

I can't do this. Faye curtsied. "My apologies, Lady Yardley, but I must go." She rushed past her.

"Clive, what has happened?" Lady Yardley insisted.

Faye ran outside and across the yard, calling Geoff.

"Do not speak to me."

"It was a mistake—"

He turned on her, his green eyes intense and cold. "A mistake that it happened or a mistake that I saw it?"

"Geoff!"

"Don't!" He snapped. "I guess it's my fault in the first place for talking you into the courtship. It's not like you didn't warn me from the start the depth of your affection for him."

Faye let out a strangled cry. "But things changed."

"Then why did you do it?"

"I don't know."

"So things didn't change enough."

"I didn't actually—"

"Oh, come on, Faye!" he yelled. "Even if that were true, the intent was there. If I hadn't walked in at that second, I might have never known."

Faye pulled at her hair. "It was a mistake."

"Would you have told me?"

"Probably," she stuttered. "I don't know. I can't imagine keeping something like that from you."

"But you would have tried?"

"I don't know! I don't know what I was thinking. I wish I could take it back. That's the only thing I'm sure of."

Geoff started walking again, and Faye rushed after him.

"Through all this, the one constant was I loved you," Geoff said. "It was like that when we began, and it was the one thing that never changed. Even now—" He stopped. "I told myself you'd never hurt me," he whispered. "You took it way past hurt. I can't see or talk to you."

He began walking again, and Faye didn't run after him this time.

She sank onto the grass and stared after him until he disappeared over a distant hill.

CHAPTER 26

The Storm

Faye

A MESSAGE ARRIVED for Faye that night from Geoff.

*Miss Faye Armstrong,
I release you from our courtship as you have achieved what you sought when we first began.
Mr. Fitzpatrick*

Faye let out a wail as Aunt Bonnie entered her room.

"What I wouldn't give to set time back and listen to you," Faye cried out. "Why would I do this to Geoff? What can I do to make him believe me?"

Aunt Bonnie put her arms around her. Her aunt had never divulged to Father and Aunt Chelsea how Faye's courtship with Geoff had begun. Faye had told them the whole of the story when she had arrived home earlier from Yardley, along with the most recent developments. Aunt

Chelsea seemed to take the news in stride. Her father's reaction was more like what Aunt Bonnie's had been, but where Aunt Bonnie's disappointment was tinged with anger, his was colored with despondency, which deepened Faye's guilt and melancholy.

"I think you should get some rest," her aunt said. "Things will look clearer in the morning."

"I can't possibly sleep now."

"Child, you're exhausted."

"I'm heartbroken, and it's all my own fault."

Aunt Bonnie sighed. "You can't do anything tonight. Either sculpt or go to bed."

Sculpt. That's a good idea.

*****

Faye stood in her studio, staring at the bust of Geoff. The moon was full and large tonight, and she had many candles lit around her.

She swiped her face. *He let me in, and I betrayed him to his brother.* The stab of guilt was so palpable she doubled over.

I know him. The bad and ugly. The so very good and trusting.

She straightened. *I must finish the piece. I'm the best person to do it.*

*****

Geoff

Geoff boarded the ship in London. He barely knew where it was going. He just needed to be out. To forget the picture that replayed in his mind of Faye and Clive. To forget Clive altogether.

*****

The rocking of the boat was unlike any Geoff had ever experienced as the storm raged. He had been down below, but as the area quickly filled with water, he crawled up to the deck. Or what was left of the deck. Half was swamped with water. The other splintering. A piece of the mast fell by him, and he grabbed on as half of the ship he was on lurched upward. He held on for dear life as it sank into the black depths of the ocean.

CHAPTER 27

Shipwreck

Faye

"AUNT CHELSEA, CAN I HAVE that extra set of China you never use?" Faye called.

Someone walked into her room.

"Did you hear—" Faye stopped short. "Aunt Bonnie, what's the matter?" She was pale and looked unsettled, which was an unusual state for her.

"How can I say this?" She frowned. "Have a seat, dear Faye."

Faye's heart started thumping.

Aunt Chelsea raced in. "Did you tell her yet?"

"What's wrong?" Faye insisted.

Aunt Bonnie guided her to the bed and sat beside her. "Mr. Geoffrey was on the roster for the ship that was wrecked at sea earlier this week. The word is all were lost."

Faye froze. "That can't be."

Aunt Chelsea sat on the other side of Faye and put her arms around her.

Faye shook her head vigorously. "You must be wrong."

"I'm so sorry, Faye," Aunt Bonnie said.

"But we can work things out," Faye cried out. "He just has to come back to me. We'll marry and have a lovely home and fill it with beautiful children."

"Faye," Aunt Bonnie said quietly.

Papa stood in her doorway.

"Papa?" Faye shrieked.

He looked sorrowful as he shook his head.

*****

Several weeks later, Aunt Bonnie entered Faye's studio looking flustered. Faye sculpted constantly, spending time with the small piece of Geoff she had left.

"Duke Hartwell and Lady Mariah are here to call upon you."

Faye stilled. They were the last people she expected to see. "I'll be there directly."

I'm sure they'll be none too pleased with me. Faye took off her sculpting uniform quickly. *It's not as though it's undeserved.*

Faye entered the drawing room and curtsied deeply. "It's an honor for you to call upon me."

Lady Mariah rushed her and grabbed her hands. "How are you?"

Faye blinked at her. "Surely you must be furious with me."

"I was shocked and grieved when I first heard," Lady Mariah admitted. "But your feelings for Geoff were quite strong. I'm sure Clive, the selfish, awful being that he is, must have forced himself upon you or somehow put you in a terrible position—"

"Mariah, I can't allow that," Duke Hartwell interrupted. "Clive would never force himself on any young woman." He glanced at Faye. "The other party would have to be willing."

Faye cringed and dropped Lady Mariah's hands.

"So you were complicit?" Lady Mariah asked incredulously. "I can't believe that. Your affection for Geoff was very real. I know that."

"It was. It still is." Faye's voice cracked.

"But?" Duke Hartwell insisted.

"It's none of your business," Lady Mariah said curtly to her brother. "You act as though it were all Faye's fault—"

"I don't mean to imply Clive is innocent in the least. I know my friend, and he heard plenty from me on this matter. But he didn't act alone, and there is ample blame to go around. Geoff didn't enter this courtship with the purest of motives, and Clive must have picked up on something in Miss Faye's manner to act the way he did. This disaster was long in the making."

"It's like I'm never satisfied. I was sure it was Geoff, but Clive made a couple of good points, and I thought I should be positive." Faye gave a strangled cry. "Clive and I should be stuck with each other for punishment. I just wish we'd never hurt Geoff."

Lady Mariah looked pained.

"We came to personally inform you we're canceling the commission," Duke Hartwell said.

Faye trained her eyes on the floor. "Of course. I understand completely."

"Without Geoff..." He paused. "I'll need to alter some of my plans. Did you finish the bust of him?"

"It's almost completed."

"May we see it?" Lady Mariah requested softly.

Faye led them to her studio.

The three stared silently at the bust for a while.

"He was fiercely proud of you," Duke Hartwell said.

"I can't imagine why," she whispered.

"I can," he said gently. "This is a beautiful piece of work, Miss Faye. Well done." He cleared his throat. "I'll wait for you in the carriage, Mariah." He left the room.

Lady Mariah took Faye's hands in hers and kissed her cheeks. "You may not feel you deserve this, but I'm sorry for your loss."

Faye nodded, unable to speak, and Lady Mariah took her leave.

*****

It took some strength, but Faye cradled the bust as though it were the man himself as she stood in the great room at Yardley. "I know what you must think of me, but I wanted to give you the bust of Geoff that he had commissioned."

His parents looked at one another, surprised.

"Geoffrey requested you do a bust of him?" Lord Yardley asked.

"Yes," Faye replied. "He never told you?"

Lord Yardley shook his head.

"You didn't tell them?" Faye asked Clive.

"No," he answered from the corner of the room. "That was Geoff's business."

"It's fitting he trusted you with such a task," Lady Yardley said.

"He should not have trusted me at all." Faye busied herself with setting the bust on a nearby table and carefully removed the sheet.

Lord Yardley stilled as his wife gasped. "It's perfect," she whispered.

"I'm glad you're pleased with it." Faye curtsied. "I'll take no more of your time, and it was very kind of you to receive me."

"Faye!" Lady Yardley grabbed her hand as she rushed by. "You loved my boy very much, didn't you?"

"I do," she whispered.

"That's all I needed to know," Lady Yardley said.

Faye curtsied again and left the room.

CHAPTER 28

Solace or Settling

Faye

ONE MONTH SLOWLY churned into the next.

Though Clive spent considerable time with his parents after their anger towards him subsided, he was at Spalding more than he'd ever been tending to his business ventures. Yardley without Geoff just wasn't the same.

Faye passed the winter in Liverpool with her grandfather, where she finished and presented his bust. She finally learned how to be steadier in purpose, though the lesson came at a heavy price.

She had just come in from doing sketches at the docks when the housekeeper informed her that Grandfather Sabo was in the parlor with Lord Spalding.

Faye's breathing stopped for a moment.

"It's good of you to join us," her grandfather said when she entered the room. "I know you were working on your sketches."

"I didn't wish to be rude," Faye said quietly as she took a seat, wishing she'd stayed on the docks longer.

"You look well," Clive said to her.

"Thank you."

Clive appeared older, like the events of the last few months had beaten the last vestiges of young manhood out of him.

"Lord Spalding and I have been discussing business," her grandfather explained. "I may sell some of his goods in my shop."

Faye relaxed a bit. A business trip would make this visit more comfortable. "That sounds like an equitable arrangement."

"Mr. Sabo, would you grant permission for me to have a private interview with Miss Faye?"

Her grandfather glanced at her. Faye swallowed and then nodded.

"Permission granted," he replied stiffly. "I'll be in my office."

Faye watched him leave the room.

"How have you been?" Clive asked.

"As well as could be expected. And yourself?"

"The same."

"How are your parents?"

"They move on with life."

"As did we all."

They sat in silence.

"I know I'm not Geoff," Clive said. "But we might find solace in one another."

"What are you proposing?"

"A courtship."

Faye shook her head. "It's too soon for me to court anyone, and what would your parents think? Surely, they'd find the idea repugnant."

"I believe repugnant is too strong. They were never truly angry with you, perhaps just disappointed.

They laid the blame mostly on me and even somewhat on Geoff. To them, we acted in an ungentlemanlike manner and endangered the reputation of a young woman. I've never seen them so infuriated with me for so long."

"People will talk."

"They'll talk anyway, no matter what we do. Most of it has subsided, and few knew in the first place."

Faye stared off.

"To be honest, I believe my parents half expect it," Clive said. "I ruined your reputation; I should put forth every effort to right that wrong."

"Is that what this is?" Faye asked quietly. "I'd rather not be married to a man who believes the union is only his duty."

Her heart plummeted. *To be stuck in that kind of marriage for the rest of my life...*

"You know I care more than that," Clive said softly.

Faye sighed. He was correct; it wouldn't be a cold, mechanical relationship. But it might not be love either. Imagining being with anyone right now was exhausting — she had nothing inside to give.

But maybe Clive was offering to help make her whole again, which would be a marked departure for him, and perhaps he was begging for the same from her. "When I saw the picture of you and Geoff in the Galleria, I'd told Geoff you were cute little boys."

"Yes, back when I protected my little brother. Somehow I've morphed into this creature I am now."

"I've never seen you as morphing. You've always been Clive to me."

He smirked. "So I've always been this awful?"

"Clive."

"I'd told Geoff you're one of the few people who understood me."

Faye glanced out the window beside her. She did care for Clive, just not in the way she had grown to love Geoff. But maybe that would change in time. "Yes, maybe we can comfort one another."

*****

Faye entered her grandfather's office later that afternoon. "You wished to see me?"

"Yes, please sit."

Faye took a seat in front of his small wooden desk.

"Lord Spalding has informed me that the two of you plan on beginning a courtship in the near future."

Faye nodded.

Grandfather Sabo studied her.

"Do you dissent?" Faye asked.

"I'll be frank; I do. Is this not the same gentleman who compromised your reputation?"

"I compromised my reputation."

"With a great deal of help, it would seem," he retorted. "And now, to assuage his conscience, he offers courtship and marriage. I suppose I could be happy that, at least, he has a conscience that prods him in such a direction."

"It wouldn't be like that. He'd offer a comfortable life."

"A comfortable life?" Grandfather scoffed. "I know that's not what you sought, Faye."

She looked away.

"Why are you settling?"

A flare of anger rushed through her. "It's better than facing a life of degradation and contempt."

"There will always be others seeking to lower you, but the second you believe it, you're done. Never forget you are valued and protected."

"By you and mine, yes. But the reality is many do not hold that view. Would you have me live here and hide out for the rest of my life when I have the opportunity to create my own household?"

"Yours?" he exclaimed. "Its very creation is being dictated by the society which seeks to shut you out. Do not underestimate your worth."

"Lady Yardley told me the same thing."

"Did she?" His features relaxed a bit as he walked towards a window. "The Fitzpatricks seem an interesting family."

"I believe they find some of the expectations of their station confining."

He snorted.

"Grandpapa," Faye gently chided. "It's nothing like the hardships or injustices you endured, and the Fitzpatricks, in particular, would never pretend or claim that. But that doesn't mean they aren't bound to anything or no one."

He tapped his fingers on the windowsill. "I see the point you're attempting to make."

"I thought you liked Geoffrey."

"I did. He seemed a stable and independently minded gentleman, and I believed his affection for you was genuine."

"It was."

"But he used you, Faye."

"He liked me, and I wouldn't have noticed him otherwise."

"I can't believe that was the only way to gain your affections."

"Perhaps not. But it's the path he took, and he did disclose to me, in time, the difficulties he was having with Clive and apologized for the position he had put me in. I had knowledge, and I was absolutely using him to my own ends, though with his consent, in the beginning."

He sighed. "The whole situation was and still is a mess, but it does no good to rehash it. And that error in judgment certainly didn't warrant the end he came to."

Faye swallowed, a rush of emotion coming upon her suddenly and unexpectedly.

"I'm sorry, Granddaughter," he said gently and looked out the window a moment. "I have no real say in this matter other than the responsibility to write your father of the developments. My only concerns were for your happiness in this decision to make what you deem a smart marriage. I don't know Lord Spalding well, and since you and your father have been closely acquainted with the family for years, I would defer to his and your judgment on that topic. I'm confident in the end you'll choose wisely."

CHAPTER 29

Can't Marry You

Faye

FAYE AND CLIVE QUIETLY BEGAN a courtship by letter in May and informed their families in June. There was no outward opposition, but no one seemed overly excited either. Both families accepted the news as fact and went on about their lives.

Faye still sought to fill a void that steadfastly remained. She traveled to Lyme for the summer with Daisy and a couple of acquaintances who still enjoyed and sought her company. The sea was pleasant, but Faye remained out of sorts, even with Clive's letters.

She was at a tea shop staring out the window when a sight made her freeze.

"Geoff," she whispered.

Mumbling something to her friends, she ran outside and frantically looked left and then right.

But he'd been swallowed up.

"No!" she wailed. *I can't lose him again.*

Faye ran to her right, dodging people. She caught a glimpse of him.

"Geoff!"

He stopped but didn't turn.

She sprinted and nearly careened into him. He was a touch gaunt, but otherwise, the same. She bent over, trying to catch her breath. "Where have you been?" she gasped out and then burst into tears.

Geoff sprang into action, guiding her to a nearby bench.

She lost it completely, unable to keep the sobs from coming. Finally, the tears slowed, and she could breathe again.

"Cornwall," he said.

"What?"

"You inquired where I was. Cornwall."

"But the ship... we heard everyone on board was lost."

"A few of us survived. The storm wasn't far off land."

"Why didn't you send word or something?"

He looked away. "I needed to be alone."

Faye swallowed. "But your family was heartbroken. Your mother..."

Geoff winced and then stared straight ahead of him. "Are you married?"

Faye played with her hands. "No."

He studied her. "But you are with Clive?"

She exhaled. "We thought you were dead."

"I was very much alive the last time I saw the both of you."

Faye cringed. "I'm so sorry." Her voice cracked. "You have no idea."

They sat in silence.

"Are you happy with him?" Geoff asked, all the fight gone from his voice.

Faye shrugged.

He stood. "I wished it could have been with me, but if you're truly happy, then that's enough. Have a good afternoon."

"Wait!" she cried out as Geoff started to walk away. "You can't just leave!"

"What would you have me do?" he exclaimed.

Faye sputtered. "Come back with me."

"To do what?"

"To at least see your family. I can understand not wanting to see Clive or myself. But your parents are shells of themselves."

Geoff closed his eyes.

"I know you think Clive has all the light and glamor, and perhaps, in a way, he does. But please believe me when I say your family has fallen apart without you. You are the glue and strength." Faye stopped, her control slipping. "I'm not unhappy with Clive, I suppose, is the best way to describe it. We're just simpatico for good or for bad. But I was one with you."

Geoff finally looked at her.

"I threw that away for a selfish, childish notion, and I'll always regret that. But please don't let my and Clive's mistake divide you from the rest of your family."

"I promise I'll call then. Just to let them know I'm well."

Faye stood. "Geoff, you don't know how glad I am to see you. How much I missed you." She swallowed. "Ached for you."

Geoff pressed his lips together. "Then it's good you had Clive to help you through that difficult time."

Faye shut her eyes as they became hot with pressure.

"Goodbye, Faye."

When she opened her eyes, he'd disappeared.

*****

Faye was back at Oakes Hollow by early September and working on the unfinished bird sculpture when Clive came to call on her. She inquired if he'd mind terribly sitting in the studio while she worked, as she'd just begun a particularly tricky section of the wing.

He settled himself with a book in the same spot Geoff had stood when he'd requested Faye do his bust. A lump formed in her throat as she looked down at the bird sculpture — the very one he'd turned over in his hands as he declared, with that sunshine smile of his, that he wanted to be a patron of the arts.

A deep wave of grief washed over Faye as she stepped back from the piece. Clive was fine consolation, and she should be satisfied, something she thought she'd never be when she had made such a grievous error. But with Geoff alive and well in the world...

It all seems so wrong.

Faye rubbed her arms from a sudden draft. *This feels like another trap when I was trying to escape a previous one. I need to be free from this as well, but now I may really lose everything.* "Clive, I can't marry you."

He chuckled, turning a page in his book.

"I'm in earnest," Faye insisted.

Clive stilled and then looked up. "I don't understand."

"I can't marry you, so we should end our courtship."

"Why? What's happened?"

Faye bit her lip. Geoff never showed, and she hadn't breathed a word about seeing him. "I'm not in love with you."

"But you have everything I wanted in a wife, and as a bonus, marrying you would be like marrying the best mate I could ever have."

Faye made an odd half snort, half laugh. *I must save us from each other. It wouldn't be the scenario Grandpapa had feared, but it's not the life I'd reached for either.* "And I want my husband to be the best mate I ever had. But don't you want a wife who's head over heels in love with you?"

"I do. So you're telling me that's not you?" he asked carefully.

"Are you head over heels for me?"

He studied her for a moment. "I must confess that I'm not."

Faye closed her eyes and shook her head. *Classic Clive.*

"But I do like and care for you a great deal," Clive rushed on. "I thought we were happy as we were."

"We are, in a way, but it's like we stayed stuck at twelve years of age together, Clive."

He chuckled.

"And while there's a wonderful type of comfort in that kind of friendship, I don't think I want that in my marriage."

Clive sat back in his chair. "That's not how you felt with Geoff?"

"In part, yes. We were friends, and it was comfortable. But I was grown with Geoff."

"Not that I didn't try hard to get you away from him, but then why did you jeopardize that?"

"I don't know, and maybe I never will. I fault others for not valuing me, and yet I seem to not see it myself sometimes. There were times I doubted I was good enough for Geoff."

"And as penance, you settled for me?"

"As penance, you settled by offering to me, probably figuring you got off fortunate."

Clive snickered and then sobered. "I'm sorry I ruined what you had."

"We were all playing games, and in the end, we all got hurt."

"True. Though one of us can rest from their mistakes."

Faye looked away. She wished to comfort Clive on that point at least, but she also wanted to respect Geoff's wishes to handle matters in his own way in his due time.

"You were always good enough for Geoff. It just took his offer to force me to view you as something other than a great playmate," Clive said. "He's the fortunate one, especially after the way we treated you."

Faye gave him a small smile. *Classic Clive.*

He sighed. "Our marriage was supposed to give me some worth. Mariah thinks I'm evil incarnate."

"I don't think it's that severe. She just wishes you were more serious."

Clive gave her a curious look. "She told you that?"

"Yes, I told her she should consider the last man on earth she'd ever think to court."

Clive roared with laughter. "And I was the man. Well, that's something to distinguish myself with. She's fortunate because a prim, stuck-up, doesn't know how to take a jest—"

"Clive."

"I don't care if she's a duchess; she'd be the last woman I'd court. I'd told Geoff she'd be good for him." He paused. "Strange conversation, as we just ended our courtship."

Faye rolled her eyes. "Do you wish to stay while I continue sculpting?"

"I do, unless you want me gone. I still prefer your company more than anyone's besides Richard." He paused. "And Geoff."

Faye gave him a soft smile. "Then please stay."

Clive smiled back and opened his book again. Faye returned to her bird, feeling more free than she had in a long time.

CHAPTER 30

A Trip for T.H.E.T.A.

Faye

FAYE WALKED into the drawing room and curtsied. "Lady Mariah, what a pleasure."

It was the end of September and a completely unexpected visit. Faye was preparing to write her grandfather back.

"The pleasure is all mine. I have a request of you." Lady Mariah handed Faye a letter. "We'd like you to go to Derbyshire and do some damage control."

Faye wrinkled her brow. "Damage control?"

"I'm afraid my brother is about to make a serious error, and we'd like you to make sure the additions at the mill are safe."

"I wouldn't know how to make that assessment. And who is the we of which you speak, if it's not you and your brother?"

"Myself and Lady Corwyn. I'd hoped Geoff had spoken to you about the work he was doing, and I know you were at a couple of their meetings."

"I was, and he did," Faye replied. "But not in any great detail, and my attendance was for a different matter. Why are you concerned? What's happened?"

"I overheard a conversation between my brother and Lord Thurston's foreman. The foreman had concerns about the safety of the work conditions for the so-called improvements they made."

"That's serious, but I'm not making the connection between it and my involvement."

"Please take a moment to read the letter."

The letter was from Lady Corwyn. She apologized that she couldn't meet Faye in person to request her assistance, but she had recently given birth to her first child.

'It's imperative things are sound at our mill,' Lady Corwyn wrote. *'I'd like to give my husband, Lord Vaughnryd, assurance everything is safe, stable, and done with the utmost care. If he has any reason to believe something is wrong, he'll pull out.'*

Lady Corwyn asked Faye to pick up where Geoff had left off and work with the foreman to ensure things were sound. She expressed confidence he'd work well with her as he'd been quite agreeable towards Lady Corwyn's involvement. T.H.E.T.A. appeared to be a group of individuals willing to work a touch outside of convention, and Lady Corwyn sensed Faye would fit into that framework well.

'I greatly appreciate any assistance you can give," Lady Corwyn wrote in closing. *'I'd take care of it myself, but I'm afraid Lord Vaughnryd will suspect something. Not that I wish to do things behind his back, but I believe Mr. Fitzpatrick would have handled this matter thoroughly, so it wouldn't have been an issue. I greatly enjoyed his brief visit. Please accept my sincerest condolences, and I hope to make your acquaintance soon.'*

Faye folded the letter. "I know little about the new machines, but I understand her concerns and will attempt to finish what Geoff began. He wouldn't want a project connected with him to be mired in ill-repute or harm to others." She grimaced. "It'll also be nice to be far away."

"I hoped that wouldn't be the case but assumed it would be. So it's bad again?"

Faye nodded. "My father and family rally behind me, but it's worse this time. I don't wish to leave Oakes Hollow, but I may have no other choice than to remove to Liverpool."

"I know many wouldn't have considered ending your courtship with Clive a smart decision, but I'm glad you did it. Can you leave immediately?"

"Yes, the sooner, the better."

"Excellent. I'll travel with you, and I've made all the necessary arrangements so our journey will be comfortable."

"You're very kind, thank you."

"And I'd like my hands," Lady Mariah said. "If you're still willing to take a commission from me."

"I'm thrilled and accept." Faye left the room filled with anticipation. Her life was falling into shambles, but she wasn't ready to fall in with it.

She had things to accomplish.

*****

They would meet with Mr. Edgar Locke, Lord Thurston's foreman, and Lady Corwyn in Bath. He resided just outside of Bath, and Lady Corwyn had told Lord Vaughnryd that she wished to visit the orphanage. That was true, but it was also a convenient excuse to obscure the other errand. From Bath, Lady Mariah would return home, and Faye would accompany Lady

Corwyn for ostensibly a visit, but also for Faye to take care of business without raising too much alarm.

They met in the assembly rooms in town, and Lady Mariah made the introductions.

"I'm happy to make your acquaintance, Miss Armstrong," said Lady Corwyn. "I've heard so much about you."

Faye grimaced.

Lady Corwyn winced. "I meant with your sculpting."

Mr. Locke was a good-looking man, slightly shorter in stature than the average gentleman. "It's not very often I'm in places of the likes of these," he said.

"I spent a good deal of my youth in an institution not too far, and this is the first time I've been here. It's quite interesting."

Faye chuckled. *I suppose that's not in the best way.* The assembly rooms in London were places she'd frequent, but she'd only been in Bath once or twice. "I suppose it takes some getting used to."

"I think I prefer my quiet country home," Lady Corwyn remarked.

"You might not find it more pleasant, but I thought of escorting everyone to the mill if that's agreeable," Mr. Locke said. "Miss Armstrong could see a working operation, and perhaps everyone could observe my reservations."

"Excellent," replied Lady Corwyn. "Does that suit, Lady Mariah and Miss Armstrong?"

Faye nodded.

"This might be a good opportunity for me to depart," said Lady Mariah. She grabbed Faye's hands and kissed her cheek. "I thank you for doing this for us, and please take care. Write me your findings and developments."

*****

Faye exhaled as she took in her surroundings. "I've never seen anything like it," she breathed.

"Neither have I, and I've been to our mills," Lady Corwyn said.

Faye was astounded when they drove through the gates, for it was a much larger complex than she'd imagined. There were three four-story buildings and one that looked like a warehouse. Other smaller structures dotted the yard, and stables were on the far end. Faye had imagined a cute, tiny building with a quaint waterwheel sitting on a creek.

They were now in a room where she supposed they spun yarn and thread. The machines stretched the thread very high up, and the room resembled a forest of webs.

"I should take you to the engine house," Mr. Locke said. "Now that's a thing of beauty. If you'll follow me, we'll walk through this building to the next, where the new looms are installed, and the weaving is done."

Faye took note of a few people at the machines. "You have some young workers."

"We do; but there are other mills that hire as young as seven. A few others made a point of not hiring under ten," Mr. Locke said dryly.

"I don't see anybody here that young," Lady Corwyn remarked.

"No, Lord Thurston is uneasy with such young workers, and he left the hiring age to my discretion. I won't hire anyone younger than thirteen and prefer that they're closer to sixteen. Any school aged workers must have lessons provided in another room in the office building, and I restrict their hours."

Lady Corwyn gave him an appraising look. "There are some who wouldn't feel it'd be important for those workers to receive that kind of an education."

"True, but not on my watch."

Lady Corwyn nodded as though she approved.

By now, they'd entered the next building. It was a vast space filled with row after row of machines, and it was tight. Faye was afraid her dress might catch on something.

"Lord Thurston has a decent-sized operation here, though not the largest in the country," Mr. Locke explained. "His family has two other mills, but this is the only one that executes the entire system from processing the flax to a finished piece of linen."

"What do the other two mills do?" Faye asked.

"They are silk mills in London and Suffolk. One has been in the family for a while, and the other was newly acquired. He also had a small cotton mill not far from here but sold it." Mr. Locke exhaled. "He and Duke Hartwell are a force."

"I heard you were the man who makes it all work," Lady Corwyn said.

He smirked. "I'm good."

"Are you foreman for all those mills?" Lady Corwyn asked.

"No, that's not humanly possible as much as Lord Thurston wishes it," Mr. Locke answered wryly.

Faye chuckled.

"They each have a manager, but their duties and decision powers aren't as expansive as mine. Lord Thurston has them carry out whatever policies I adopt here, so my duties are still primarily in this mill. Recently, those duties have included incorporating the new looms into all the mills and training the workers. The punchcard automation isn't easy, and it's turning into a massive task."

"I can imagine," said Lady Corwyn. "And now there's the possibility it's not done safely when the environment is already inherently hazardous."

"Exactly. Only so many people can get through an exit at a time, especially when there's an emergency. And I'd feel better if there were some kind of water reservoir even if we sit on a water source."

"I believe I read about a couple of newer mills that are supposedly fireproof," Faye ventured.

Mr. Locke brightened. "Yes, I'd love to talk Lord Thurston into those designs. Anything that's fire-resistant would be welcome. But so far, we're only working with the existing building structures."

"Is that something Mr. Fitzpatrick had explored with regards to our mill?" Lady Corwyn asked Faye.

"The writings were in his possession, so I assumed so," she replied. "But if the addition remained a single story, I believe the efficacy of the design would have been reduced."

"I see," said Lady Corwyn.

"We can speak further in my office," Mr. Locke said. "It's noisy and dusty here on the floor."

"Why is Lord Thurston opposed to making the needed changes?" Lady Corwyn asked once they were settled in another building.

"It's not that he's opposed, per se; he just doesn't see the need to make them quickly," Mr. Locke explained. "We recently installed the fans to cut down on fluff, and he just purchased the looms. I believe he's thinking with his bank account instead of his head at present." He winced. "I apologize. That was rather impertinent."

"But accurate it would seem," Lady Corwyn commented. "Do you believe there's the same danger at Vaughnryd?"

"I wouldn't be able to say without looking at the setup or at least some drawings. From what I understand, Mr. Fitzpatrick and Lord Vaughnryd's changes were modest."

"They were," Faye confirmed. "Only two looms, and they built a separate addition for them."

"Then I'd venture to say you don't have a problem," Mr. Locke said. "But I can take a look when I'm there to train the new hires."

"Tell me about these fans, please, Mr. Locke," said Lady Corwyn.

Mr. Locke was in the middle of his explanation when a woman in a smart jacket and hat breezed in and dropped some papers on Mr. Locke's desk. "Tell your boss to stop buying and selling mills. He's messing up my curves."

Mr. Locke chuckled.

"Lady Darton!" Faye exclaimed. "What a nice surprise."

Recognition lit Lady Darton's eyes. "Miss Armstrong, this is a delight." She sobered. "I'm sorry to hear of Mr. Fitzpatrick." She exchanged glances with Lady Corwyn. "If you're ever in need of anything, you're welcome at Darton, though I'm sure Lady Corwyn has made the same offer."

"She has, and we're to journey there after we leave Bath," Faye responded. "But I thank you for your kindness."

Mr. Locke looked concerned. "Are you in any trouble, Miss Armstrong?"

Faye was quiet for a moment. "I made a serious error in judgment from which I may not recover, but no, I'm not in any immediate danger."

"She'll be quite safe with us, Mr. Locke," Lady Corwyn said.

Mr. Locke nodded and then looked at the papers Lady Darton had brought. "Please, don't tell me you're saying what I think you're saying?"

"If he spent more money, he'd make more?" Lady Darton grinned. "'Tis true. If my arithmetic is right, and it is, he hasn't hit the peaks of those curves yet and maximized. That's assuming all the other inputs and information I've been given are correct."

"We're keeping that a secret between you and me right now," Mr. Locke said.

"You don't think it would encourage him to make the changes you'd like?" Lady Corwyn asked.

Mr. Locke shook his head. "Those changes, while necessary, aren't exactly the inputs of which Lady Darton speaks. And under no circumstances is anyone to breathe a word of this to Duke Hartwell. He'll buy another loom, and heaven knows where I'll put that one."

Faye stifled a laugh due to the serious nature of this matter, but it was amusing they all seemed to have the same reactions to Duke Hartwell.

Lady Darton stood. "It's been lovely, but I rather use my arithmetic for the stars, and this little one is knocking again."

"You're with child?" Faye asked.

Lady Darton smiled. "I am, and Mr. Locke, you have a baby boy to play with."

Mr. Locke beamed. "That I do."

"Congratulations!" Faye exclaimed. "Who's your wife?"

"She was Miss Christiana Yeatman before she married me."

Faye wrinkled her brow. "Yeatman? As in shipping tycoon and one of the richest men in the country Yeatman?"

"The very one," Mr. Locke answered wryly.

Faye was at a loss. "Then why is Lord Thurston using another novice shipper when he has a connection through you to a seasoned one?"

Lady Darton started laughing.

Mr. Locke scratched his head. "It's a long story."

Faye glanced at Lady Corwyn, who wiggled her eyebrows which made Faye chuckle.

"It's a story which my wife would probably love to share if we have the pleasure of your company one day, Miss Armstrong," Mr. Locke said.

"I'd like that."

*****

Faye sat back and looked around her room. She was enjoying her stay at Vaughnryd much more than she had anticipated given the circumstances. Lady Corwyn had put her in the best guest room, which was a massive suite. The Vaughan's baby boy was charming and resembled Lady Corwyn. Faye enjoyed holding and playing with him. This part of the country was lovely too, as Geoff had told her. A pang went through her as she remembered his promise to take her to this area.

She studied the correspondence between Geoff and the architect that Clive had turned over to her before she had left Oakes Hollow. The two additional looms didn't necessitate an extra entrance by themselves, so one wasn't included in the initial plans.

Faye recalled Duke Hartwell's eagerness for more looms at the last meeting she had attended. While it was clear Lord Vaughnryd and Geoff weren't to be rolled over, Geoff's work would probably be successful, which increased the likelihood that more looms would be bought in the future.

Faye considered the plans again. *What would be needed if the space was used to its fullest? Maximized, as Lady Darton had described?*

Faye pulled out a sheet of paper and began a letter to Mr. Locke.

CHAPTER 31

The Brothers Fitzpatrick

Geoff

GEOFF HANDED THE REINS of his horse to the stable boy at the entrance of Yardley. He stood there for a moment, taking everything in. It was the beginning of October, cloudy, and everything was wet. Yardley seemed to have lost some of its glow.

He wasn't sure if that was only his perception of the place or if things really had grown somber. Faye had said his family was heartbroken. Her comments and his promise were the only reasons he was here. Despite everything that happened, it had been difficult to watch her cry, but at the same time...

His chest clenched. *I'm here. Let's do this, and then I'll decide what's next.*

The butler opened the front door and stared at him. "Mister Geoffrey," he whispered.

"Hello, Thompkins." Geoff stepped inside. "How's your family?"

"Well, sir. I thank you."

"Please tell my father I'm here. I'll wait for him in the drawing room."

"Of course, sir." He broke into a grin. "Welcome home. The sight of you does my eyes glad."

"It's good to see you too." Thompkins was a reminder of what his childhood had been. Like Molly, he'd been at Yardley for years too.

Geoff made his way to the drawing room. It was dark and felt like a tomb, which was unusual. He opened some shutters and curtains.

His father burst into the room. "Thompkins was right."

Geoff hadn't realized how much he'd missed him. "Hello, Father."

His mother ran into the room with a cry as she rushed towards him and gave him a back-breaking hug.

Geoff tried to soothe her. *Faye was right. I should have returned sooner.*

"What happened, son?" his father asked quietly.

Geoff told his parents about the voyage.

"But why are you just coming home now?" Father inquired.

Geoff bit his lip and then looked away.

His mother hit him. Hard.

"Ouch!" Geoff exclaimed.

"You boys! I can't believe you two would put Faye in that position. I had never—" She hit him again. "I was always proud of my sons until that day when I heard what had happened. Shame on you two." She smacked him on the arm.

"Phyllis," his father said. "Let's try not to scare him off again."

Geoff stared at the floor. He'd been consumed with how he'd been wronged. His mother's words were a stark reminder of the situation he and Clive had placed Faye in. "No, Mother has an excellent point," Geoff said. "I'm sorry."

"You're apologizing to the wrong person," she said stiffly.

Clive entered the room, and Geoff stifled an absurd laugh. *I don't know why I'm surprised. He was always here anyway. I guess some things never change.*

Father took Mother's arm. "We'll leave the two of you."

Mother kissed Geoff's cheek one more time before letting Father lead her out of the room, leaving Geoff alone with Clive.

*****

"You're alive," Clive said.

Geoff nodded.

"But you stayed away all this time?"

"I promised Faye I'd come and at least see Mama and Papa. She was right; I needed to make my peace."

"When did you see Faye?"

"Several months ago."

"Did the two of you make plans to resume your relationship?"

"I made no promises of the kind. Why would I do that when she's with you?"

Clive shook his head. "She broke it off. Or rather, we both agreed it'd be best for us not to marry."

Geoff stared at him. "Why?"

"We would have been jolly mates, but I don't love her the way you do, and that's the husband she should have."

Geoff set his jaw. "And you came between us anyway."

"I had no notion it was so serious until that day." Clive looked at the floor. "I wasn't blind to the fact she's an excellent woman, and you'd be very happy with her. Most likely happier than in any marriage I'd make. You always win the stuff that matters, and I couldn't take it."

"So this is what we are? Competitors instead of brothers?"

"We weren't always like that."

Geoff paused. He'd told someone that it was important to try to restore the peace. *Maybe I should take my own advice.* "I don't like competing."

"No, you never have. If I'd paid better attention, I would've realized that was a testament to how deeply you felt for Faye. You fought for her."

"I don't regret it, but I wish the battle had been of a different kind. The losses are heavy."

"They don't have to be permanent."

Geoff studied his brother.

"Why did you do it?" Clive asked, sounding perplexed and pained. "Faye might have been the ultimate goal, but you wanted to hurt me too."

"It felt impossible to get out from under your shadow."

"I thought you preferred being under a rock, and I was doing you a favor by taking some of the attention off you."

"That's true to an extent, but it seemed like you were intentionally eclipsing me, like it wasn't altruistic."

Clive sighed. "For being under a rock, you cast quite a shadow. I don't know how you managed that."

"My shadow?"

"My strikingly handsome, mysterious younger brother." Clive snickered. "Your shadow was huge. The silent manly hunter. The gentleman who never danced. Father's favorite."

Geoff scoffed. "I wasn't father's—"

"He never meant to show a preference, and I'm not saying he doesn't love me, but you were clearly his favorite. Do you know how hard I had to work to keep up? If Father had been allowed to choose, you'd inherit Yardley. You're the epitome of what people envision of that station, not me."

Never in Geoff's imagination had he seen himself in that light.

Clive started pacing. "You should go to Faye. Unless you really can't be with her anymore."

Geoff sighed. "Seeing you two together destroyed me. I didn't think she'd do that even if she had decided for you and against me."

"Ordinarily, she wouldn't have. I had to exert a lot of pressure on her to waver." He paused. "Faye wouldn't want you to go to her for only this reason, but she suffered much heavier public consequences for our actions than we did."

Geoff rubbed his face.

"Faye and I will always care for each other's welfare, but our courtship was more about survival and a desire to somehow right a wrong. Yours was not."

"It's just hard to trust again. I thought she loved me."

"She does, Geoff. Faye never cared for me like that."

"She hurt me." *You hurt me.*

"I'm not a matrimony expert, but I'm well acquainted with messing up. I know you think Faye is near perfect, but she's human." Clive smirked. "Believe me. And she'll disappoint and pain you on occasion, just like you will her. Granted, our trespass was rather large."

Geoff gave him a look.

"You'll have to decide if you can move through that," Clive said. "But it might be worth the close relationships. You think our fight would have been so sharp if we loved each other less?"

Geoff gave him a sad smile. "No, brother."

"Faye is in Derbyshire at Corwyn. You'd have plenty of time while traveling to think everything through." He paused. "And Geoff, I'm very sorry. You had me pegged. I took what didn't belong to me, and I will forever regret doing so."

Geoff nodded. "I am too. My aim was to wound you, and I find no pleasure in my success."

"You should see the bust Faye finished of you in the Galleria," Clive said. "It's a fine piece of work."

*****

Geoff entered the Galleria, and his attention was immediately arrested by the picture of him and his brother, beaming at the artist.

What happened to us? A deep sense of loss filled him. Longing. *I want that back.*

Clive seemed different now. A little more sober. A little more appreciative.

I'm different now.

I'll have to figure out a way to get us there again. Today was a good first step.

Geoff located the bust on a pedestal in front of a window framed with a red velvet curtain and gold braids. The clouds were clearing outside the large windows, and the sun played hide and find, casting moving shadows across his facial features on the sculpture.

Faye was an extraordinary artist.

The bust was perfectly him. Not just with correct physical properties, though it was a marvelous likeness, but she captured his personality. He reached out and lightly touched it. Like she had him when she'd done the piece.

He had opened up to Faye, and she had eagerly walked in, cherishing every bit of him she'd seen. The soft, joking laughter. The tension and uncertainty. The challenge.

He loved the artist, and she had seen that too.

Can I let her in again?

CHAPTER 32

Like the Clouds

Faye

FAYE LAID THE BOOK beside her as she watched the children run off. The Vaughans had arranged a retreat at Lady Corwyn's Ainsley estate for the children from the Bath orphanage while it was getting improvements. Faye had offered to assist since Lady Corwyn was with her second child. It was a breezy day, and the high, billowy clouds moved over the hills in the distance.

She was a den mother of sorts to a group of five girls. While it kept her busy without being too taxing, her escape wasn't working out quite the way she had envisioned. Many things reminded her of Geoff.

But the landscape and task was a pleasant way to hide from everyone. The wagging tongues. Judgmental looks. Remain here, and she'd hurt no one again.

A sniffling, little girl ran to Faye, and showed her scraped leg. Faye cleaned it with a handkerchief, and it looked worse than it actually was. She blew on it and kissed the girl's cheeks, and the girl ran off again.

"Crisis averted," a deep voice said behind her.

Faye stilled, and then slowly turned. "It's like you just materialize all the time," she whispered.

Geoff sat beside her. "How long have you been here?"

"Less than an hour—"

He chuckled. "No, I mean in Scotland."

"Yes, of course. A couple of weeks."

"It took some work to find you. Do you like it here?"

"I do. Ainsley is very restful. It seems to take on Lady Corwyn's personality."

"This place reminds me a bit of Yardley."

"Does it? I don't think it looks anything like."

"Yardley had always been peaceful to me. It's only in recent years that it felt less so, and that was largely my own fault."

They fell into silence.

"Did you ever see your family?" Faye asked.

"Yes."

"And?"

"I regret my absence caused as much pain as it did. I had no notion the news was as bad as that, until you said something. But I really did require time to myself."

Faye played with her hands.

"Clive told me to see you," Geoff said.

Faye swallowed. "I couldn't do it," she whispered. "Especially when I found out you were still alive."

"What if I didn't wish for us to be?"

"I still couldn't be with Clive. The chance to be with you was worth risking being alone."

Geoff seemed to watch the sky. "Breezy day."

"Yes, they're quite common."

"It's amazing how quickly the clouds move." He was silent for a moment. "I want to be like that."

Faye gave him a curious look.

"Move. Freely."

"Do you feel stuck?" Faye was perplexed.

"Yes, and I tire of it." He gazed at her. "I'm sorry."

"I was the one who erred. But I'm determined not to hurt anyone again."

Geoff gave her a kind smile. "While, obviously, I'd rather that course of action not be repeated, Clive told me not to expect perfection from you. I think it's something we could both bear in mind."

Faye studied him for a moment. "You're much more fore-bearing than I would expect."

"I put you in an untenable position by playing on your emotions, and then condemned and left you to bear the consequences. There's excellent reason for Mother to have been angry with me. Can you forgive me?"

"Of course, if you can me."

Geoff nodded. "I left you before. Can you trust me not to do it again?"

"If you can do the same with me."

Geoff took her hand. "Shall we give us another go?"

Faye stilled. "Truly?"

Geoff smiled at her. "Truly."

"I'm still here for a time, so courting may be harder."

"I think we courted enough," Geoff commented dryly. "Let's go straight for marriage."

Faye gave an uncontrollable giggle.

Geoff winced. "I apologize. That wasn't romantic at all. Would you marry me?"

Faye kept giggling.

"That was still awful," said Geoff. "I had something rehearsed and even wrote it down, but it seems worse to read a proposal."

Faye couldn't stop giggling.

"Is this so bad that hoping you'll consent is absolutely ludicrous?"

Faye shook her head violently.

"So you're accepting?"

Faye nodded vigorously, still giggling.

Geoff beamed. "That was easier than getting you to court me."

Faye finally calmed down enough to speak. "You will hear absolutely no arguments from me, Mr. Geoffrey Fitzpatrick, but unfortunately, there are no hornbeam trees around."

"We'll just have to start a new tradition here."

Geoff leaned over, and Faye had just closed her eyes when she heard giggles.

"That's not you," Geoff mumbled as he pulled away.

A group of children stood before them, snickering.

Faye sighed.

"So is this what having children will be like?" Geoff asked.

Faye collapsed into laughter.

CHAPTER 33

Plans & Accomplishments

Faye

"YOU NEVER GOT YOUR TRIP?" Geoff asked Faye when he came for dinner, two weeks before their wedding in January. Faye remained at Ainsley after the children had returned to the orphanage, and Geoff was staying with a family in a nearby village. They would wed at Ainsley and then rent the home from Lady Corwyn. When Daisy heard of their engagement in November, she set out immediately for Ainsley, and was with Faye.

The wedding would be a small affair with just their families. Such a trip would be more difficult that time of year, so they were traveling together to make it easier. Her father and aunts were surprised at the betrothal, but not at all displeased. Lord and Lady Yardley seemed more relieved than anything, and they believed this ending was the best for all parties involved.

"When Lady Helena heard about the incident and your subsequent departure, she was through with me," Faye replied. "They took another lady, and I heard the trip was a debacle and cut short. In the end, it was best I didn't go. I managed to end up in Scotland on my own accord, and the Gillinghams seemed to want a fashionable maid more than a traveling companion. I wasn't about to fetch and carry for them the whole time."

"Nor should you be expected to. I've been corresponding with your father and mine. Between the three of us, we could put together a year abroad so you can sculpt."

Faye squealed and threw her arms around his neck. "Are you sure? Won't that be horrifically expensive?"

"We'll be fine, and everyone wants to do it. It wasn't so much whether we could go; it was more a matter of what style we'd go in." He gave her a kiss. "Mother has spoken. It's to be an excellent honeymoon and art tour."

Faye squealed again.

"Mother really loves the bust you did of me," Geoff said. "You could do no wrong in her eyes."

Faye gave him a look. "That can't be true."

"She blames Clive and me for that. You're in the clear."

Faye shook her head.

*****

Geoff

Geoff and Faye were at the Vaughnryd mill to witness the first run of the two new looms the following spring.

Lord Vaughnryd held the fabric before him. "Excellent."

"Now you just need to make a ton more of those—"

Lord Vaughnryd gave Jarvis a look.

Jarvis waved a hand. "Do what you two want. I was skeptical, but this setup is nice even if it is small."

Geoff thought it was perfect. It felt good to help accomplish this, and he hadn't lost his sanity in the process. It was even better the project was something in which both he and Faye could claim a part.

The space was a simple rectangle with a wide aisle down the middle. Faye had decided to implement some of the fire resistant designs, like brick interior walls and floors and iron supports. She also included a substantial but attractive door, additional windows, a fan, and a water reservoir outside. Lady Corwyn and her had decided the addition would be two stories and added a dining hall on the second floor.

The additional features increased the cost of the addition, stretching the budget to its maximum, but Lord Vaughnryd was pleased with the results. He believed he could boast one of the best millwork environments in the area, if not the country. If he and Lady Corwyn added more looms in the future, they could move them into the space with few, if any, improvements.

"When are you planning your next shipment?" Jarvis asked Clive. "It'd be nice if we could squeeze on some fabric."

"Next month. And don't tax my shipping fellow. You already got him preoccupied with that steam craziness."

Jarvis waved a hand. "He's fine. We need to make the trips worth his while."

Even though the brothers had fully reconciled, Clive decided it would be best to stay busier with Spalding and T.H.E.T.A., and Geoff was now days away in Scotland. The extra space seemed to do them both well. Geoff was actually happy when his brother had briefly visited Ainsley.

Faye squeezed Geoff's hand. "You did a good job."

He kissed her forehead. "So did you."

"Doing the hands instead of the whole figure was Miss Faye's alteration," Mariah said.

The sculpture wasn't completed, but Mariah had grudgingly given Jarvis permission to briefly put her hands on display somewhere holding damask.

"That was a good idea," Jarvis said to Faye. "Do you have any others?"

"I'm sure I could dream some up. I heard Lady Corwyn wrote a few jingles in her time. Perhaps we could team up again."

Lady Corwyn smiled.

"I'd be delighted to hear of any other ideas you may have, Mrs. Fitzpatrick," said Jarvis.

"You can drop the missus, Duke Hartwell." Faye smiled. "Faye is just fine between friends."

Jarvis grinned. "Since Fitz insists on calling me Jarvis instead of Richard, you should too. Fitz and Faye. I rather like that."

"I do too," agreed Geoff. "Though I'm partial to Mrs. Fitzpatrick."

Clive gagged. "Married people."

"It's not a problem you'll need to contend with in the foreseeable future," Mariah said dryly.

"Nor you," Clive retorted. "I expect a full report on spinsterhood in ten years."

"Play nice," Jarvis crossed his arms. "I don't want to hear it the whole way home."

"Just put the duchess in a different carriage," Clive said airily.

Mariah gave him a dark look.

"Nothing like family," Faye whispered to Geoff.

Geoff laughed and squeezed her hand.

Epilogue

7 years later

Geoff

"JARVIS IS HAVING a house party," Geoff informed Faye off-handedly.

"Oh!" squealed Daisy. "You got an invitation! It's all anyone has been talking about in London."

"Really?" Geoff asked disbelievingly.

"I should have known you would," Daisy said. "You two are practically family."

After marrying Faye, Geoff really tuned out of social items except for their closest acquaintances near Ainsley. He and Jarvis regularly corresponded, and they would visit one another on occasion, but Geoff didn't keep up with the mundane tittle-tattle of their set. True to prediction, Geoff's role turned into pulling back and checking Jarvis so the other members of T.H.E.T.A. didn't hurt him when his ideas and requests got too ridiculous.

Daisy had just arrived from London two days before, traveling to Ainsley as the season drew to a close. Still unmarried, she had decided to live in the London house and visit Oakes Hollow and Ainsley regularly. She appeared to enjoy her freeness since she had no husband or family and possessed the income to support a comfortable lifestyle.

"So I guess we're going?" Geoff asked Faye.

"Of course. The social invite of the year? Not only are we going, but we're show-stopping."

Geoff groaned. Generally, Faye was relatively modest given their income stream, but every once in a while she wanted to pull out all the stops. It looked like this trip may be one of them. He didn't actually mind too much, for a decked out Faye was definitely something he enjoyed.

"But we have to bring Daisy," Faye continued. "We can't leave her here."

"I don't want to impose," Daisy said. "I can return home when you go. Hartwell isn't that far from London."

"Come with us," Geoff insisted. "Jarvis won't mind."

"You think the aunts would be willing to care for Lily while we're gone?" Faye asked Daisy as she bounced their two-year-old daughter on her lap.

"Are you joking?" Daisy answered. "Between those two and your father, you may never see your baby girl again."

Geoff may be partial, but their daughter was adorable. She looked like Faye with green eyes and just as lively too. Faye's father and aunts visited them at Ainsley once a year, and they couldn't get enough of Lily when they were visiting last summer. The Armstrong siblings seemed to be three peas in a pod at Oakes Hollow.

Faye

"Would you like me to speak with Lord Vaughnryd about continuing at Ainsley once they leave?" Geoff inquired.

"They're not to stay?"

This year was supposed to be the Fitzpatricks' last at Ainsley, for the Vaughans had planned to live there the following year to oversee the opening of their new orphanage and school. Faye and Geoff had discussed buying property to establish their own estate but had never really gotten around to it.

Geoff shook his head. "I just received a letter from him yesterday. They now plan on staying for one year and then renting out the place again to help pay for the school. He said we could even remain while they're here, but I believe that'll be a bit tight."

The Vaughan brood was large and busy. Lily was in between the Vaughans two youngest children.

"Lily might enjoy all the playmates," Faye said. "We could consider a little time here with them."

"Let's plan on a few months at Yardley and Oakes Hollow, and then return to Ainsley and visit with the Vaughans."

Faye nodded vigorously. She loved being with Geoff and Lily up here, and after all the drama with her and Geoff's courtship, it was nice to be with people who knew little of their past or family. And she liked the Vaughans immensely. They reminded her a bit of her own family whom she did miss.

"I'll write Lord Vaughnryd immediately of our plans," Geoff said.

Faye squealed. She had been sad about leaving Ainsley, but knowing it would be temporary lifted her again. "We're quite the nomads."

Geoff chuckled. "As we're wandering, you can consider who you'd like to select as our next artist in residence. It's your turn."

Faye loved this almost as much as Geoff. They've had three so far. The first one had been a female landscape painter that Geoff had hired to do his hornbeam painting that hung proudly in their bedroom. The second was a gifted violinist. They just finished with the last student, a young boy of poor means who lived nearby and worked in the stables. He drew startlingly excellent likenesses.

"I can't wait to visit Oakes Hollow." Faye kissed Lily's fat cheek. "You have lots of history in that part of the world, little one."

"We should arrange a visit to Grandfather Sabo as well," Geoff said. "If we're showing Lily history."

Faye beamed. He hadn't met Lily yet. "Absolutely."

<<<>>>

We forge on

When Lady Orelia Maddox meets the blacksmith, Duncan Reid, at his family's forge, neither one is aware of their families' entangled past. All Orelia knows is she's never met a man like Duncan, and he's convinced a woman like her will land him in trouble.

As an unlikely arrangement and partnership blossoms into something more, a series of events unfolds that test what each of them thought of their worlds and families and whom they should trust.

A disaster claims the life of one of T.H.E.T.A.'s own, forcing each and every member to question their ambitions, loyalties, and priorities. For some, it will lead to painful conclusions and decisions, others new and decisive trajectories. But everyone must forge ahead in a way none of them had predicted.

T.H.E.T.A. will go through the fire. Will it be destroyed or galvanized into something stronger?

PROLOGUE

Edgar

Silence descended upon the tiny room as Mr. Edgar Locke shifted in his chair.

Mr. Reginald Grant frowned. "I usually get my machinery through Lord Broughton."

"No one with T.H.E.T.A. can deal with Lord Broughton," Duke Hartwell informed him.

Lord Thurston scowled. "I read the bylaws. Nothing was written about excluding Lord Broughton from contracts."

"We'll discuss later," Duke Hartwell said to him and then turned towards Mr. Grant again. "That's my final offer."

Edgar swallowed the sour taste in his mouth. He was more closely acquainted with Mr. Grant because their fathers had been land agents in the same neighborhood. He had an urge to stand up for him.

It was early April, and they were at a small lodgings house in the village of Meldon. Duke Hartwell had requested the presence of Edgar and his employer, Lord Thurston, on a tour of Mr. Grant's mill and a meeting following. After touring, the duke had offered Mr. Grant a way out of his troubles, but to be eligible for that assistance, Mr. Grant's operations must be brought under the house of T.H.E.T.A. This involved ending his contracts with his current vendor and revamping his mill with the looms Duke Hartwell was pushing. Edgar understood requirements, but those seemed high-handed, especially for a man with few options.

Mr. Grant was a well-to-do merchant, though his affluence, at present, was in danger. The bank that had financed his mill had suddenly gone under, and he had recently lost a shipment of cotton at sea. The town was also giving him push-back on how his works diverted the river water.

"I don't have a choice." Mr. Grant sighed. "You have a deal."

"Excellent. I'll speak with some people to see if we can get the town off your back in the short while. Lord Thurston, can we contact the engineers you use?"

He nodded.

"Good. Maybe they can develop a new system for Mr. Grant's power. I'm making arrangements to execute the loom modifications, which should decrease the price a great deal. I just need to find a suitable blacksmith. And Mr. Locke, if we could press you into service by reviewing Mr. Grant's operations and tighten things there—"

"You can speak with me about that too," Lord Thurston cut in. "I don't particularly care for you ordering around my foreman."

"Of course. Gentleman, I'm off. Mr. Grant, I'll be in touch to draw up the appropriate paperwork." Duke Hartwell was gone with a gust of wind.

The three of them sat quietly.

Edgar had been inclined towards Duke Hartwell when he'd first met him as Lord Manton. He had struck him as a bright, energetic gentleman with a keen eye for clever ideas. He was still those things, but his energy and drive were slowly morphing into obsession — one that involved besting Lord Broughton. Edgar didn't understand from where all this emanated. Originally, T.H.E.T.A. was about getting brilliant innovation out there, which Edgar wholeheartedly embraced.

"It's not all bad, Mr. Grant," Lord Thurston said. "At

least you won't lose your home and mill."

"True, but I feel I paid more than money to do so."

Lord Thurston stood. "I must return. I'll see you Monday, Locke."

"Let's get dinner, Mr. Grant," Edgar said once he had left. "The place across the way has savory eating."

*****

They were starting their meals when Mr. Duncan Reid entered the establishment, and Edgar invited him to eat with them.

On occasion, Edgar took the two-day trip to Reid's Forge to have work done for the machinery in Lord Thurston's mills. The Reid family's expertise was better than that in Bath and rivaled some found in London. Reid's Forge was also smaller than most in the cities, making the experience more personalized, so it was worth the trip.

Duke Hartwell's words flitted through Edgar's mind regarding the need for a blacksmith. Mr. Reid would fit in with T.H.E.T.A., not only for his skill, but he looked the part too, and that would subconsciously be important to Duke Hartwell. The blacksmith had brown hair and eyes and possessed a robust and well-conditioned physique.

"I seldom see you in this neck of the woods," Edgar remarked after Mr. Reid told the serving boy his order. "What brings you here?"

"I dropped off an important order for my father," Mr. Reid replied. "This place was on the way back. Are you still foreman?"

"I am."

"And still at Thurston?" Mr. Reid inquired.

"Yes, but I moved into the steward's house on the estate. I'm married now and have a young son and daughter. You?"

"Still on the family land and at the forge. Recently reached Master Blacksmith status."

"My congratulations for years of hard work coming to fruition," Edgar said. "Are you staking out on your own or remaining with the family?"

"My father is grooming me to take over."

Edgar studied Mr. Reid. The blacksmith reminded him of a sun that could competently and constantly hold planetary bodies in position around him. Edgar desired that kind of power from someone in his own orbit. "Would you be interested in becoming a member of an alliance?"

"A blacksmithing one?"

"No. Textile. You'd be an excellent addition."

Mr. Grant snorted. "Be careful, Mr. Reid. I'm not sure I'm pleased with what I've gotten into with the duke, though I trust Mr. Locke."

"I thought you worked for Lord Thurston?" Mr. Reid asked Edgar.

"I do, but I'm also a member of T.H.E.T.A., and that's Duke Hartwell's brainchild."

"One of the farmers that frequents the forge said his brother's fabrics were undercut by the duke's brocade linen," Mr. Reid commented.

Edgar grimaced. He was aware of those reports. When Edgar had brought the matter up, Lord Thurston had expressed it wasn't his brocade, and their product was doing fine, so he was unconcerned.

Duke Hartwell didn't personally own any mills, but strictly speaking, T.H.E.T.A. owned a few. The holdings comprised of silk and linen mills mostly in the greater London area and surrounding counties nearer to where Duke Hartwell resided. The only two outside that locale were a linen mill nearer to where Mr. Reid hailed, and now Mr. Grant's mill.

"Lord Thurston allowed you to do both enterprises?" Mr. Grant asked.

"He's not completely aware of the situation yet."

Mr. Grant chuckled. "It's the first I've heard of you not being completely loyal to Lord Thurston. The Lockes are as integral to Thurston as the family itself."

Edgar shrugged off a twinge of guilt. Their families had always coexisted well. Edgar owed his excellent education and employment to Lord Thurston's father and had always gotten along well with his son, who was now marquess. But that very tie was the reason he threw his lot in with T.H.E.T.A. Perhaps it was the effect of marrying and having children of his own, for he was tired of generation after generation of Locke being tied to Thurston. Serving.

"I'm allowed to invest my money where I please," Edgar said.

"An investor?"

"I can't afford much; I'm barely a drop, but Duke Hartwell allowed me to do so in addition to operation assistance."

"That won't create a conflict of interest?" Mr. Reid questioned.

"It hasn't yet, and Lord Thurston's operations are part of the alliance."

"But he's not invested?"

Edgar shook his head. "He had no desire to be that heavily entrenched, and was only looking for an edge in materials, machinery, and advertisements."

"What happens when your operations assistance involves a rival mill?" Mr. Grant asked.

"There are limits," Edgar replied. "But an alliance should minimize the rivalry between members."

"What does Duke Hartwell know respecting limits?" Mr. Grant muttered. "It might be cozy now, but there may come a day when the members are less than friendly, and the alliance becomes an alienation, especially if it wasn't created carefully in the first place."

It unnerved Edgar to hear his concerns voiced so clearly. That was another reason he sought to be more involved.

"I'll exercise care." Edgar glanced at Mr. Reid. "It'd be nice to get blood in there that didn't run so rich."

Mr. Reid nodded. "Tell me about this T.H.E.T.A."

CHAPTER 1

The Business of Marriage

Orelia

"Remind me why we're watching this game of badminton instead of participating." Lady Orelia Maddox readjusted her position in the chair for the hundredth time, losing the battle of appearing interested.

Three pairs of men played a short distance from them on the vast green at Kengsley. She enjoyed a vigorous game of badminton, but this one was painful to watch since none of the gentlemen involved were spectacularly skilled. It was a late Monday afternoon, and Orelia rubbed her arms in a weak attempt to gain warmth.

"They want to show off," one of the ladies replied. "And I, for one, don't mind watching the show.

"My suitor is the best one out there," commented another.

Orelia agreed he actually had a little skill. It was all for nought, however, since his partner couldn't maintain a decent volley.

"I propose we find a couple of rackets and a shuttle-cock and get to work." Lady Louisa Oram said. "Show these men a real game."

Orelia hopped out of her chair.

"You can't play," their hostess exclaimed. "It would completely destroy the scene."

Orelia sat down, remembering the real reason they were gathered — a painting the Beaumont siblings had commissioned for this 'scene'.

"Did you admire that move, Lady Orelia?" called the Beaumont brother.

Louisa smirked. "You better be careful when you stand, my friend."

"He's a fine-looking gentleman, is he not?" their hostess, and his sister, asked Orelia.

He wasn't the nicest of men, so Orelia wasn't excited, but she smiled politely back. "He is."

"What do you think of him, Louisa?" another lady inquired.

"He's too smooth for me. I prefer a hint of awkward-ness."

"Let Mr. Luke Notley be your man," their hostess remarked. "He's plenty awkward."

The other ladies chuckled as Orelia frowned. Mr. Notley might not be the most dashing of young men, but he was kind and thoughtful. Traits that seemed sparse amongst the company here.

"Mr. Notley disapproves of me." Something in Louisa's tone hinted that she cared more about that than she ordinarily would.

"Did you not court Lord Arlen?" another lady asked Louisa. "He struck me as the smoothest of gentleman when I saw him in London."

"We did court for a short while, and though I wouldn't describe him quite the same way, his company was immensely enjoyable. But you see, I did not marry him."

Louisa had looks Orelia envied with glossy, dark brown curls and deep brown eyes. Orelia's lean frame wasn't unattractive, but she preferred Louisa's plumper and more shapely form. Orelia's looks, though compelling, never captivated the way her best friend's did. Ash-blond hair, dark gray eyes, and fair skin, Orelia resembled a cool, overcast day as opposed to Louisa's bright, colorful, whip-them-up presence.

Louisa managed to get in and out of situations on a regular basis, but she didn't seem serious about marriage at the moment. Orelia loved her friend, but her brother's choice of wife was a wise one.

"Instead, that Teresa Barclay managed to snatch him up," the lady remarked. "It's a wonder that chatterbox could—"

Their hostess cleared her throat loudly and gave a significant nod towards Orelia as the others laughed softly.

The lady winced. "Forgive me. I forgot they were connected to you. They are a fine pair all the same."

Their hostess exhaled and turned towards the painter. "That'll be all for today. We'll resume tomorrow."

Two days down, four more to go.

*****

"Yes, Father." Orelia curtsied and stood in front of his desk in the study. She had arrived home from Kengsley three days ago.

Horace Maddox, Earl of Rexley, was an arresting man of sixty-one, remaining fit and healthy through the decades. The only thing that betrayed his age was his snow-white hair, which gave him an air of distinction rather than maturity. His authoritative manner made many careful to cross him.

To his children, he never inspired such fear and tentativeness. Orelia didn't have difficulty being around her father and found his presence safe and comfortable. The mother of her older brother had passed away the year after his birth, and her own excellent mother had died four years ago.

Papa leaned back in his chair. "I'm in the mood for a ball. Are you up to planning one?"

"Of course. Tell me what particulars you'd like included, and I'll handle the rest." *I'll rope Teresa in this one. She'll be thrilled.*

In all honesty, Orelia was growing tired of planning endless social engagements, but her father seemed eager for this one, and she liked pleasing him. Orelia enjoyed the company of others and being active, but she didn't aim to fill her life with parties. The trip to the Beaumonts had been a bit trying, so she would rather have a rest before becoming involved with another. Orelia suspected this ball had ulterior motives, which further dampened her excitement.

"How did you enjoy your stay at Kengsley?" her father inquired.

"It was satisfactory."

He chuckled. "I haven't heard that kind of description from you in a while. None of the gentlemen pleased?"

"There were a few ladies there, Papa," Orelia teased.

"Yes, of course, but we all know what the actual game afoot was. Lord Kengsley didn't improve upon closer acquaintance?"

"No," Orelia replied flatly.

Her father chortled. "I didn't think he would. Are you still set on not going to London this season?"

"I'm not in the proper humor for it. It's best I stay home."

"That could be a smart move too by encouraging greater interest and curiosity."

"Papa, you do realize my every action isn't part of a larger plan to get married."

"Certainly. You're not as single-minded as that, but it would ease my mind if you were more motivated. I hope to see you settled before I die."

They chatted for a while longer, and then Orelia returned to her room. Appearances and protecting the family line were important to Papa, so he was eager to secure that and her happiness. Orelia was fortunate that she should be financially provided for, whether she was married or not.

The business of marriage...

*****

Teresa Maddox squealed. "I'd love to help you plan the ball!"

Orelia figured that would be her sister-in-law's response. Teresa loved dances, socials, and clothing. Picture-perfect appearance featuring light brown hair and warm brown eyes with a personality to match, her disarming and engaging mannerisms had drawn her older brother, Pierce. Orelia liked her sister-in-law a great deal, and Father loved her.

"The gang still the same at Kengsley?" asked Pierce.

"Unfortunately," Orelia replied dryly.

He snickered.

That grouping wasn't their inner circle, and she eagerly anticipated spending time with her closest friends during the winter.

She and Pierce had always gotten along well. They had similar looks, except his eyes were turquoise instead

of her gray. Their temperament and viewpoints tended
to be alike as well.

He would inherit Rexley and become an earl upon
Papa's death. Until then, he was in charge of another
estate of Papa's, Arlen, and lived there with Teresa. Arlen
adjoined Rexley to the east, which made visiting convenient, and Orelia did so frequently. It didn't have the
imposing, fortress appearance of Rexley. Instead, Arlen
was bright white and newly redone in what they called
the Italiante way, which seemed to be increasing in popu-
larity. Pierce loved it.

Teresa was precisely the woman Orelia's father had
wished would be mistress of Rexley again and bring
it back to a happening splendor. She was a hospitable
hostess and had already made Arlen a fashionable place
to be invited. Teresa was a felicitous fit for Rexley and
Arlen, for her former home, Archer Hall, was not dis-
similar to Rexley. Their fathers had some similarities in
personalities, though Orelia considered her father the
warmer and sociable of the two. Teresa's father was quite
taciturn.

"Duke Hartwell will arrive in time for dinner," Pierce
said. "Are you available to stay?"

Orelia perked up. "I am."

Teresa grinned. "I'd imagine you'd find his company
more agreeable."

Orelia did. She, Pierce, and Louisa have known
Hartwell since childhood. He was handsome, full of
energy, and always engaged in some ambition. His
station was perfect — close enough to be in the same
sphere, but his was sufficiently high that marriage would
elevate her status and pocketbook. The Maddox family
was wealthy, but Duke Hartwell was more so. If she had
to rely on a gentleman for her income, it might as well be
ample.

"Hartwell is well suited for you," Pierce remarked. "Should I do some nudging?"

"Thank you for the favor, but a woman has her pride. I'll nudge if I'm so inclined," she said loftily. "Besides, Duke Hartwell has courted no one since that unfortunate business five years ago."

"You could be the woman to entice him from his cynicism," said Pierce.

As Teresa and Pierce discussed the evening's menu, Orelia's mind drifted towards Hartwell. There was no reason not to think on him. His existence paralleled hers except for the business aspects, in which he seemed absorbed. But it was unlikely he'd involve her in those. Round after round of social engagements stretched before her when she contemplated a life with him.

"Orelia?"

She started. "I'm sorry, Pierce. Did you say something?"

"Daydreaming about Hartwell?"

"Not in the way you imagine. Why is everyone in a hurry to marry me off?"

"You don't wish to be married?" Teresa asked.

"I do, but it's not my goal in life."

Pierce gave her a contemplative look. "What would you say is?"

"I don't know." *What do I want out of life?*

She had the uncomfortable feeling it wasn't what she was currently doing. The business of marriage seemed perhaps a profitable but unfulfilling enterprise at present.

*****

As expected, Hartwell arrived not long before dinner. He was a man of twenty-seven years with very dark hair and eyes.

"What brings you to this part of the country, Hartwell?" Pierce asked.

"I was in Meldon closing a mill deal, and wished to visit before continuing to Vaughnryd."

"We're glad you did. Vaughan mentioned you're doing a lot of mill closings," Pierce commented. "I thought you were only distributing the loom?"

"I'd always envisioned offering a whole mill experience. Since Spalding had talked me out building my own, piggybacking on others was the next best thing." Hartwell turned towards Orelia. "What have you been about, Orelia? I heard you were present for the latest Beaumont display of pretension."

She chuckled. "I was there, and it wasn't that vexing."

"So only half wretched then."

"Louisa was present, and we can always amuse ourselves."

"Yes, Louisa is exceptionally accomplished in that area. What gentleman is her latest flavor of the season?"

"Duke Hartwell," Teresa chided.

"I can't even defend her on that score," Orelia said. "But she's on a streak. No suitor since this past fall."

Hartwell did a mock gasp. "She didn't pair with anyone at Vaughnryd this past winter?"

Pierce snickered. "Her choice wasn't inclined to pair with her."

"I must meet this gentleman!" Hartwell declared. "Any man strong enough to fend off Lady Louisa Oram is worthy of being knighted."

"You three are horrible!" Teresa exclaimed. "Honestly, Orelia, your best friend."

Orelia shrugged. "Louisa has voiced the same sentiments herself."

"You've met the gentleman," Pierce said to Hartwell. "A Mr. Luke Notley."

"Notley?" Hartwell repeated. "Louisa fancies him?"

Orelia nodded. She had forced Louisa into confession while they had been at Kengsley.

"He's a capital fellow!" Hartwell exclaimed. "I met him a few years ago at Eamon. There may be hope for Louisa yet. I hope she's serious. I'd hate for his affections to be trifled with."

"He's no lightweight," Pierce assured him. "Louisa will not be trifling with any of his affections if she can catch them in the first place."

"Good for him. This will be excellent for her," Hartwell predicted. "Speaking of getting caught, I hear you're quite elusive, Orelia."

"As are you, Hartwell. Someone can easily catch me, but it takes the right bait."

Teresa winked at her and mouthed, "Nice."

The main course was served, and everyone busied themselves with eating. It was hard for Orelia to swallow her food. She wasn't sure she wished to encourage Hartwell for he seemed happy as he was.

And Orelia found she was happy with that.

CHAPTER 2

The Blacksmith

Duncan

Duncan Reid's eyes opened before dawn, as they always do. It was Monday morning, a week following his trip to Meldon for the delivery. He endeavored to be at the forge earlier so his aging father didn't have to rush. Duncan could also work uninterrupted before customers started arriving, and they needed to close on time because he was attending a gathering later that evening.

He rolled out of bed, the wooden frame groaning under his moving weight. Duncan washed and dressed in a white shirt and vest, his typical work outfit. Father required them to look neat, but the clothes got dirty and scorched. He tossed water over his head and finger-combed his hair.

The Reids resided on the outskirts of a small village that was a couple of miles from a larger town. Duncan lived in his parent's first house, a three room, single story, thatched roof abode nicely framed with trees as it sat at the edge of the woods. It was a sturdy and quaint home that Duncan kept clean and simple. His own dwelling, favorable reputation, and master blacksmith status gave him excellent credibility in town.

He gobbled down his breakfast and headed to the forge. Sometimes he drove his wagon in, but when able, he enjoyed the pleasant thirty-minute walk as the day dawned.

His family's blacksmith shop was on the edge of town. When his younger sister, Sarah, had finished her apprenticeship, Father decided to enlarge the shop to give them and their customers extra room. The original building was an attractive brick structure, and he had adjoined a smaller secondary space with another forge, a small office which doubled as a storage room, and an open area with large glassless windows to make it easier to speak with customers. His father's operation wasn't the large scale of many of the city guilds or ship forging enterprises, but the three of them, a journeyman, and several apprentices made things tight at times.

Duncan put on his leather apron and got the fires going. It were as though everyone's plow broke at the same time, so they were now inundated with repairs in addition to the regular rounds of sharpening. That wasn't his favorite task, but it paid decent money. He preferred the projects that involved creating mechanical objects or crafting something more ornate.

Duncan had just finished a sharpening job when his father, Leonard Reid, came in. "Morning, Duncan. Excellent."

"Morning, Father."

Duncan's father was smaller than him and had what many described as a wiry strength. He put on his apron and scanned the list of orders for the day. "I'm seriously considering taking on another apprentice. Mr. Black was inquiring for his youngest son."

Duncan was surprised. "Are you positive?"

"I want to ensure you have the assistants you need when your sister and I aren't here."

In the recesses of his mind, Duncan knew that his father would not work the forge in the near future. His mother had him and Sarah later in life, and his father was angling towards not working anymore or at least a lot less. Duncan hoped Sarah would continue, as he was proud of having a sister blacksmith. But that would depend on her marriage, and Duncan was never sure how much she enjoyed this, though it was clear she appreciated the different kind of independence having a trade gave her.

Their forge was essentially it for a large area. His father stepping down would leave him to fill an enormous responsibility.

*****

Duncan carefully laid the rose he'd finished on the anvil in front of him. It was painstakingly detailed work, and he had been bound in the deepest of thought for hours completing it, losing track of time.

While he enjoyed this task more than most, he was concerned his father may have oversold his talents on this request. Mr. Briggere of Wingate recently had his kitchen and drawing room refinished, and he desired new pieces to match. Duncan was tasked with making the flower decorated andirons and the somewhat complicated crane contraption for their new second hearth.

If he could pull it off, it'd give the forge bragging rights, as work of that level was typically only found in the city groups. Mr. Briggere was willing to pay handsomely since it saved him a lot of correspondence or a trip to London.

"That turned out nicely," Sarah remarked, looking up from the skate blade she was finishing.

"I only need to do it three more times."

"Maybe he'd be okay with just two and a fancy vine decoration."

"Father promised him four, so I'll deliver four." Duncan indicated towards the skates. "Who ordered those out of season?"

"Lady Arlen requested skates made for herself, her sister-in-law, and Mr. Briggere's step-daughter so they could try skating next winter when they traveled back to Derbyshire and the lake country. The winters have become so cold as late, it's apparently become quite popular again."

Duncan snorted. "Popular with people who have time whirl around on ice?"

Sarah gave him a look.

"It does appear to be a better way to amuse than others I've seen and heard." Duncan studied the skates closely. "I see you adhered them directly to the boot."

"It's recommended according to what I read on the matter. Then they don't have to keep re-attaching the skate. I could make us a pair if we could spare an extra set of boots."

"I'm not buying boots to wear only a few times a year."

"I suppose you're right, and that's wise. But it would be diverting."

Duncan didn't disagree, but that was bordering on frivolities for which they didn't have the money. While not frivolous herself, Sarah seemed keen on the activities of the upper classes, which was a vast departure for his family. She was twenty-two and very bonny with blue eyes, like their father, and dark brown hair. Every so often, Duncan wished he could give her some of the niceties and experiences of that station, but he was personally quite content with the world into which he had been born.

Duncan was taking off his apron at the end of the day when his best friend, Timothy Linton, came in. His frame reminded Duncan of an inverted triangle, for his friend had a small waist but broad shoulders. He was as tall and strong as Duncan, though extremely slender, almost bony. "We're going to Kipps tonight, right?" he asked.

"That's still the plan."

From time to time, someone in town or the village hosted a dance. Tonight would be a larger gathering because the Kipps owned one of the public buildings rented out for larger assemblies. They usually threw three a year, and their venue was conveniently located in the village instead of town.

At the gatherings, the food was tasty, company entertaining, and Duncan loved dancing. He preferred the lively dance at the halls, where people and couples really moved, not the namby-pamby stuff his mother had taught him when he was younger.

"Lona asked if you'd be there," Tim said.

Lovely Lona. They'd been doing not serious for a while now. She wasn't what he'd envisioned in a wife, but if they went on like this much longer, they'd be talked of as flirts, which wasn't a reputation Duncan cared for. Maybe he'd bite the bullet and ask to court her.

Tim fiddled with one of the fire pokers. "Is Sarah going?"

"Why don't you ask her?"

Duncan believed Tim fancied his sister, even though he hadn't confided in him on the subject as yet. Sarah was particular with men for she knew her mind, and unlike many females her age, could actually make a real income.

She came out of the forge area. "Fires are out."

"The sweet and beauteous Sarah," announced Tim. "Every day I behold your shining face is a blessed one."

Duncan snickered. Sarah's face was indeed shiny from all her sweat, and there were streaks of ash across it.

Sarah gave them both side-eye. "Will you be long, Duncan? Or should I go ahead home?"

"You can leave. I have a few things to finish up here, and then I'll lock up."

"Will I gaze upon your magnificence this evening, fair Sarah?" asked Tim.

"I may reconsider going," she replied. "I'll see you at home, Duncan. Tim, I hope no harm befalls you."

"You're my angel, so I'm sure none will," Tim called.

Sarah rolled her eyes and walked out of the shop.

"You're ridiculous," Duncan told his friend. "Let me finish up so we can get out of here." He grinned. "We have a gathering to dazzle."

*****

For its location in the center of a small and simple village, Kipp's Place was surprisingly fashionable and large. By the time Duncan and Tim had arrived, the evening was in full swing, and they headed to the dining section first to eat.

The hall had a few auxiliary rooms, but most of the structure was a massive open space with high rafters and sectioned off with large pillars. Several long tables were set with food, so guests could eat. They had assigned a few younger girls to keep the food coming.

"They went all out tonight," Tim commented as he dumped a huge spoonful of mashed potatoes on his plate. "It's been ages since I've had these."

The boys dug in.

"Sarah looks especially fine," Tim remarked.

Duncan glanced at her on the dance floor. He supposed she was extra attention-getting tonight. He didn't think he'd ever seen her in that dress before, and it was a shade of blue that made her eyes stand out.

"Are you going to ask her to dance?"

Tim speared his food. "Don't know."

"Are you going to sit there and look like a kicked puppy all night?"

Tim scowled at him.

"If you actually talked sensibly to her, she may return your interest."

He gave Duncan a furtive look. "Are you all right with me fancying her?"

"Of course. Why wouldn't I be?"

Tim shrugged. "Sometimes fellows don't like it when a mate is after their sister, and I understand that."

"If you were a scoundrel, I'd beat you, but you're fine. Better than fine. I can think of no man I'd rather her be with."

Tim grinned. "Thank you. You don't know how relieved I am to hear that."

"Why aren't you serious with her?"

Tim snorted. "The Miss Sarah Reid? She'd never consent to court me. At least if I act like a dunce, the rejection hurts less."

Duncan shook his head. "Suit yourself. She's mortal, like the rest of us."

"I know, but Sarah is a remarkable woman."

"And you're a remarkable guy."

Tim had been known as the child with the hare-brained ideas when they were younger, but he'd grown into a steadfast man and still had a jolly sense of humor. He was a talented, hard-working carpenter and had earned himself an excellent reputation and a decent wage. More than a few young women wouldn't mind courting him. Sarah would probably consider him, but he'd have to make it known he was serious.

"Would you like me to put in a good word for you?"
Duncan asked.

"If you think it'd help."

"You're a respectable and agreeable guy." Duncan
clapped Tim's shoulder. "Any girl would be fortunate to
have you. Sarah has a problem if she doesn't see that."

Lona slid into the seat next to Duncan. Wild curls
matched her personality, which Duncan had found
exciting at first.

"I have the next dance free," she said.

"Sounds good," Duncan replied. "Let me finish
eating."

Lona left.

"What are you and Lona doing?" Tim asked.

"Don't know."

"Are you going to act like a cornered hen all night?"

"I'm not cornered."

"If you don't do something real tonight, you may
be."

Duncan pushed himself back from the table. "I'll set
things straight. Maybe now before we dance, in case she
wants to find another partner."

A few minutes later, Lona seemed puzzled as they
stood outside the back of the building, the sounds of the
gathering faint. "I'm fine with that."

"Fine with not courting?"

"Yes." She grabbed his hand. "Let's go. They're
beginning the next dance."

Duncan stopped her. "We need to modify our
behavior then."

"So now you're only dancing with girls you're
courting? Are you turning into a stuffy, old noble?"

"No, of course not. But we don't act like just the boy
and girl on the next farm either."

"I know, and that's how I want it." Lona gave him a
wicked grin and dragged him a few steps.

"No, we can't do that either."

Lona pouted. "What's wrong with a few kisses?"

"Nothing if we were serious."

Lona exhaled. "Fine. Can we dance now? Or is that too close?"

Duncan chuckled. "Let's dance the night away."

*****

Hot and sweaty, Duncan took a break from dancing. The room was loud, as many had freely availed themselves of the ale. Usually things didn't get raucous, but Duncan remained alert since it was a larger crowd, and he wasn't as familiar with everyone. There were out-of-towners in attendance. He, Tim, and Sarah were seated with a few of them who recently had orders finished at the forge.

"My blade seems odd." One of the farmers gave Sarah an even look. "Is that one you worked on?"

Her eyes flashed.

"I did that work," Duncan answered tightly. "Is there a problem with how it's cutting? It was all right when I tested it out."

The man cleared his throat. "No, Mr. Reid. It's lighter than I'm used to."

"I tried a different alloy mixture I read about. The lighter blade should be strong enough to cut efficiently but slow fatigue."

The farmer lit up. "Right good idea there."

"Sir, if you're to question another's work in company, you better have grounds," Tim said.

"Of course, Mr. Linton. I meant no disrespect to the girl."

Tim scowled. "Miss Reid is a full-grown woman and a professional."

"Yes. Miss Reid." He stood and gave her an awkward bow. "I think I'll get more ale."

Sarah's face was still twisted as he walked away.

"We don't have to take orders from him anymore," Duncan said. "I'll speak to Father about it."

"No, it's fine. We're the only option for miles. But Father can deal with him and do his work. Don't do him any more favors."

"Done."

Sarah thanked Tim and then hopped up. "I think I'll find a partner and dance my angry energy off."

"Will I do?" Tim asked, looking unusually serious and intent.

Sarah hesitated, her cheeks turning a little pink. "Sure."

Duncan wiggled his eyebrows at Tim as he guided Sarah to the dance floor.

CHAPTER 3

A Visit to Reid's Forge

Orelia

Two days later, Orelia rubbed beneath her spectacles and threw her pen down. Papa was definitely trying to pair her off. This guest list wasn't even trying to hide the fact. It was almost as obvious as the company at Kengsley.

How embarrassing.

Orelia glanced at her sketches, fighting the urge to work on them, for if she began now, she'd be lost in her drawing world for hours. Instead, she left her room and ran down the stone steps of the old castle to take a ride.

She exited the castle proper and crossed the courtyards towards the stables. The family had designed the yards with gardens and a large fountain to be inviting, though the original purpose and layout of Rexley didn't lend itself to that.

While the stable master got her favorite horse ready, Orelia engaged him in light conversation. "What will you do the rest of the day?" she asked.

"Go into town to speak with the blacksmith," he replied. "The horses require new shoes."

Their manor supported a charming town bustling with activity, and the nearby village was positively quaint. Orelia loved going into town and sometimes journeyed unattended and incognito. Her father would have a fit if he knew she went in as often as she did, especially without company.

I'm desperate for something new and unusual to do. "I'd like to accompany you."

The stable master's face grew blank. "I don't think that's advisable, Lady Orelia. Lord Rexley would disapprove."

"He generally doesn't object."

"The business with the blacksmith is important and will occupy my full attention. I'd be responsible for your safety and harshly dealt with if anything should happen." He paused. "Though ultimately, you could order me to take you and the discussion would be closed."

"I'd rather not, and if it's to come to that, then I'll remain behind."

He appeared resigned. "If you come, please bring one or more house servants to accompany us."

"Done."

On her way back inside, she made a mental list of the places she'd like to stop: *the bakery for treats, maybe a new pair of gloves at the shop, and I'm definitely going with the stable master to the blacksmith.*

Neda appeared in Orelia's bedroom five minutes later. She was a couple of years older than her and had been a governess with an influential family in Kent. When the daughter had married and Neda had lost her post eight years ago, Orelia's father inquired if she could be a companion and maid for Orelia at Rexley. It was an excellent pairing.

"Are you quite determined to go to the blacksmith shop, Lady Orelia?" Neda hesitantly asked after Orelia explained the situation.

"I'd never been, and think it'll be interesting."

"Would your father approve?"

"Why is everyone, all of the sudden, overly concerned with my father's approval?" Orelia exclaimed. "As lord, of course, it's of concern, but I'm well over age and not without my own authority."

Neda curtsied. "Of course, Lady Orelia. Please excuse me, but I'd hate to see any strife between you and your father." She paused. "And I confess myself."

"I don't wish to get you in trouble, but I see no reason he'd disapprove. It's an uncommon place for me to visit, but that heightens its appeal. I've been to other shops in town, and he's never voiced consternation."

"That's true. I'll fetch my things." Neda curtsied again and exited the room.

Thirty minutes later, Orelia returned with her companions.

"Let's be off then," the stable master said.

*****

Duncan

Duncan wiped the sweat from his brow. It was mid-afternoon, and in a couple of hours, they'd end work for the day, as it took time to shut down properly for the night.

"Look alive, son. The stable master from Rexley approaches." His father's normally relaxed face appeared tense.

Father hated the earl who lived there, Lord Rexley, but they received a steady and robust business from the estate. His servants were fine to deal with, so the Reids were obliging when they came. Duncan never understood his father's ill feelings; it was so unlike him. But he figured there must be good reason and so acted respectfully and intelligently but remained guarded. He straightened his clothing and stood next to his father as he greeted the stable master at the windows.

There were two ladies with the stable master, and that was out of the norm. The brunette stood apart, appearing to be one employed at Rexley as opposed to a visitor or family. She was attractive so Duncan gave her a smile, and she returned it cautiously.

The other lady was animated, looking around and listening in on the conversation the stable master had with Father. She was pretty as well, but then Duncan supposed most ladies of nobility would have the time to make themselves so, and there was no way she wasn't one. She had the look down to perfection, one of cool elegance which her manner at present belied. Her eyes shone as she asked Duncan's father a couple of questions. Hair escaped from an expensive looking hat that matched the dress she wore.

At one point, his father called for Sarah. "Answer any questions the lady might have."

The lady's eyes grew large as Sarah appeared from the forge room and joined them at the window. "Are you a blacksmith?"

Sarah grinned. "I am."

The lady's eyes grew wider, which Duncan didn't think was possible. "But you're a woman?"

"That I am, milady."

The men claimed Duncan's attention again as the lady fired questions at Sarah.

✳✳✳✳✳

Orelia

Orelia regarded the young woman before her with wonder. *She can't be much younger than me but can work with iron. She could probably earn her own living if she must.*

"Can you make door knockers?" Orelia inquired.

"I surely can," Miss Reid replied.

The blacksmith mentioned her name was Sarah. I'll have to remember that. Orelia flicked her head towards the men standing with the stable master. "Is the blacksmith your father?"

"He is."

"And the man standing with him is your brother?"

"Yes." Miss Reid smirked. "Do you like the look of him?"

Orelia felt flushed. "Do not speak such nonsense."

"I beg your pardon, milady." Miss Reid was still smirking.

Orelia bit her lip. Miss Reid's brother wasn't like any young man in her acquaintance. He possessed larger arm and shoulder musculature, possibly due to his profession. Sarah's brother commanded attention and held it, his demeanor and looks put together to suggest a certain amount of gravity without being cheerless.

He caught her eye, and she felt flushed again and looked away.

"Would you like to speak with him?" Miss Reid asked.

Orelia cleared her throat. "We haven't been properly introduced."

Two minutes later, Miss Reid had demolished that excuse.

Mr. Duncan Reid gave her a mischievous grin and then he bowed. "A pleasure. If you will excuse me, I have iron to forge."

He walked away, chuckling, and Orelia stared after him. She wasn't used to being teased in such a manner, especially by a young man. She was accustomed to them paying her a great deal of deference. Sometimes too much, which made her sick, but deference all the same.

The stable master took the young man's place before her. "My business here is done, so if you are ready to depart, we can meet the cook in the food market."

Orelia's mind whirled as she considered Miss Reid. "I may have a project for you in the future. I'll be back."

"I look forward to your return."

Orelia gave Mr. Duncan Reid one last glance.

He caught her looking again and tipped his head.

Orelia grew warm as she pivoted and walked off with the stable master and Neda. She shook her head. *Regain control. You're a countess and don't need to be a blushing schoolgirl in front of a tradesman, of all people.*

*****

Duncan

Duncan tossed a tool on the ground. *Messed up another shoe. Blasted lady, blew my mind to bits, especially with that last look.*

If a woman of his class had gazed at him like that, he'd call on her the next day. But Lady Orelia was definitely out of his station. *Any dealings with her will land me in trouble.*

That shouldn't be difficult as she was unlikely to come back. *Today was a chance meeting that'll never be repeated.*

The Women of T.H.E.T.A. series

Amid the British Industrial Revolution, players are taking their positions, and new battles are beginning — between individuals and within families, companies and industries, generations and their ideals. Relationships and loves are lost, old ones galvanized, and new ones forged.
Modern heroines
Unconventional heroes
Meet the women of T.H.E.T.A.

T.H.E.T.A. Books

Expanding Their Scope - The Women of T.H.E.T.A. Book 1: Abigail
Who Is Madalene? - The Women of T.H.E.T.A. Book 2: Hannah
The Hunt - The Women of T.H.E.T.A. Book 3: Rebecca
Sculpting His Likeness - The Women of T.H.E.T.A. Book 4: Faye
Forge - The Women of T.H.E.T.A. Book 5: Orelia

T.H.E.T.A. Novellas

The Foreman - The Women of T.H.E.T.A. Novella: Christiana (prequel)
The Imagination Room - The Women of T.H.E.T.A. Novella: Deanna (A Dr. Fiske story)

Future T.H.E.T.A. Books

The Ruins - The Women of T.H.E.T.A. Book 6: Mrs. Locke
Woven from Manipulation - The Women of T.H.E.T.A. Book 7: Jocelyn
TBD - The Women of T.H.E.T.A. Book 8: Portia

C.E.J., writing as Elizabeth Borae, resides in Pennsylvania, U.S.A. Besides writing, she has also worked as a literacy and mathematics tutor, specializing in working with children who have learning challenges. With a B.A. from Rutgers University majoring in Economics and Art History, she attempts to inject a little business into her stories about relationships and family during a period she loves in art and literature, the 19th century.

www.ingramcontent.com/pod-product-compliance
Lightning Source LLC
Chambersburg PA
CBHW061231210726
48293CB00003B/730